PAPERBACK VERSION

ISBN-13: 978-0615915616
ISBN-10: 0615915612

To order additional copies of this book, contact:

Cover design by: AMB branding design

www.ambbrandingdesign.com

shauntakenerly.wix.com/shaunta-presents

shauntakenerly@yahoo.com

Please leave a review

Nicole Michelle

Chosen

By: Nicole Michelle

Nicole Michelle

KENERLY PRESENTS

for Nevaeh Nicole

Nicole Michelle

"Do one thing every day that scares you" –
Eleanor Roosevelt

KENERLY PRESENTS

ACKNOWLEDGEMENTS

I would like to thank God for blessing me with the talent to communicate both verbally and in writing. I've always wanted to write since I was eight years old starting with poetry. Although I have been blessed with so many different talents, the gift of writing is by far my greatest gift, and I feel so blessed to be living one of my many dreams. I thank God for my life and my daughter's life. Nevaeh Nicole is the greatest blessing besides my own life.

I would like to thank my family for being here for me whenever I needed any of you. Some of you all were great support, and I sincerely thank the ones that believed in my dreams as much as I did. It is far too many of you to personally name, but I love, cherish, and appreciate you all.

I would like to thank my aunt Wanda J. Jenkins for turning me onto horror and thriller novels and movies as a young child. She sparked my interest in otherworldly things.

I would like to thank Shaunta Kenerly for working with me and giving me this opportunity. I thank you for believing in my work almost as much I do. I sincerely thank you from the bottom of my heart.

I would like to thank my best friend Rhonda Allen for everything. You have been the best sister and friend I have ever known.

You give me so much insight and offer me a different perspective on life in general. Your wisdom is well beyond your years and your advice is the best ever. You understand and appreciate me. I love you girl, I thank you for all that you are, and for being here for me anytime.

I would like to thank my friend Qiana Morgan for being such a great friend to me. I can never repay you for the long talks, the insight, and all the love you have shown me in such a short amount time of knowing me. You are a great person, and I am so very blessed to be friends with someone like you. I hope we remain friends until our lives expire.

I would like to thank everyone that has purchased a copy of this book for your support. I hope you enjoy what you read, and I sincerely appreciate you. I also encourage you to check out my other novel <u>Beyond Day's End.</u>

CHAPTER ONE

Glossy, tired eyes reflected the large curtain-less window like a mirror. Rays of light, bright yet concentrated dimmed in response to the setting sun. The colorful foot-prints across the sky left thin trails of clouds soon to disappear within the darkness of the night. Jordin, a second year senior, and victim of the surrealism of her own mind, crept toward the window. Her black high heel biker boots clucked and echoed with every slow step.

Her breath continuously fogged the window then dissipated a few seconds later. Her long dark brown hair eclipsed her line of sight as she tucked it behind her ear to no avail. Her hair slipped from the comfort of the crease where the ear attached to her head eclipsing her line of sight yet again. Blowing her hair out of her face she held her hair up as a temporary ponytail holder. She turned and quickly looked behind her. The cold silence in the hallway raised the hairs on the back of her neck.

Jordin turned to the window and peered out, as she always did, removing her hair from blocking her line of sight yet again. Michael stood outside of the residence hall speaking with some students. His hair cut short and his face had no facial hair with droopy yet bright eyes. Jordin's eyes protruded and her heart rate hastened. She held her breath as she stepped out of sight pinning herself against the wall the window posted. Her hands trembled as she gripped her purse tightly. She peered out of the window. Michael had vanished.

The elevator dinged loudly echoing in the silence of the hallway starling Jordin. The elevator doors opened as Mira stepped out. Jordin remained pinned against the wall as her breathing was shallow and rapid. The elevator doors closed.

Mira asked, "Jordin are you okay? You look terrified."

Jordin giggled, "Nah girl, I'm fine. I'm just tripping, you know?" She peaked out of the window again.

Mira temporarily rested her hand on her hip, "You went to that sorority party didn't you?"

Jordin stared into her pale blue eyes, "Yeah, why?"

Mira caught her purse from slipping from the crest of her shoulder trying not to drop the two textbooks she held firmly within her grasp, "Rumor is someone laced the drinks with PCP. A girl at the party was rushed to emergency. You might wanna get checked out. PCP causes hallucinations."

Jordin smacked her lips as her sharply arched eye brows grimaced, "For real? I didn't hear about that," her smoky voice dryly muttered.

Mira rescued her long frizzy sandy brown hair from underneath the strap of her pink purse then flung it across the back of her shoulders, "It's true. Been buzzing around campus all morning. There's gonna to be an investigation."

Jordin glanced away from Mira, "Thanks for lettin' me know."

"You missed the elevator. Are you going down?"

Jordin glanced out of the window, "Eventually. Trying to make sure I have everything."

Mira raised her eyebrow and nodded her head, "Guess I'll see you later."

Jordin nodded her head in agreement. Mira walked down the short stretch of the hallway before turning the corner on her way to her dorm room. Her two inch high heels hollowed as they clucked the floor with each shallow step.

Jordin peered out of the window again catching her hair from blinding her in search of Michael. Where did he go? How did he know? She didn't see him anywhere as her heart rate slowed and her muscles relaxed. She gave a sigh of relief as she rubbed the back of her neck smirking. She combed her hair with her fingers then gently rubbed her eyes without smearing her bronze eye shadow as she collected herself, *I'm scaring myself. I need to calm the fuck down.* She popped her neck then her knuckles then pressed the down button on the elevator.

An unfamiliar girl stood next to her. Her clothes dirty, ragged, and smelled exceedingly bad; a mixture of underarm funk and trash. Her hair was ear length, slicked back, and dirty. The girl's non-arched eye brows, droopy eyes, and sharp features gave her a masculine appeal. Jordin knew the girl was not a student but felt pity for her although she secretly wondered where she came from. She cleared her throat, "I have some long johns, some sweat clothes, and a quilt if you need to stay warm out there."

The girl stood without saying one word; her body rigid and cold; her attention towards the floor. Jordin slyly scratched her nose with her hand covering her entire nose, "Well unh...I have a couple dollars if you hungry."

The girl didn't say anything, an awkward silence. The only sounds in the hall were the girl's heavy breathing and muffled voices from people talking loudly in the dorms down the hall. Jordin cleared her throat, "Going down?" Dorm room doors slammed shut as Jordin's muscles tensed. The girl stared blankly at the elevator in an inexpressive tone, "Cheaters always win but whores pay the price."

Jordin grimaced stepping away from the girl towards the window, "Excuse me?"

The girl grabbed Jordin's arm and yanked her towards her; nose to nose. She

mumbled in a deep, masculine voice, "You."
She snarled.

Jordin screamed, snatched her arm from the girl, pushed her down then ran down the end of the hall opposite the dead end of the window she stood next to. The girl chased her as the elevator dinged and the doors opened.

Jordin ran down the hall continuously looking behind. The girl bent down on all fours, hands and feet, behind her as her green eyes turned black. The lights in the hall flickered then dimmed. Jordin ran hastily as her clacking footsteps clacked three times every second filling the silence of the hall. As she looked behind, the girl climbed on the wall and ran behind her quickly moving like a cheetah. She opened her mouth revealing sharp teeth like that of a shark as saliva dribbled from her mouth while she roared like a male lion.

Jordin turned the corner of the "L" shaped hallway coasting down the longest hall towards the stairway clenching her purse. The girl turned the corner behind her on the wall. She ran down the wall onto the floor leveled with Jordin. Jordin burst through the exit door passed the other set of elevators. The door smacked the wall as she missed the first step tumbling down the first level of stairs bumbling and fumbling landing on her side. She slid against the wall of the landing opposite the doorway. She dropped her purse and cell phone. Stiff, bruised, and achy, she got up and ran, limping, down the second level of stairs skipping steps - cluck, cluck, cluck, every second. The girl leaped down the entire first level of the asymmetrical "u" shaped staircase onto the landing like a flying squirrel; thudding as she kept her balance. Jordin sighed as her eyes moved frantically.

Jordin hopped down the stairs onto the landing with the girl only a half of flight behind her. The girl's footsteps sounded sticky and wet. Jordin soared down all of the stairs from the landing onto the next floor, stumbling as she landed. The girl ascended down behind her onto the landing on all fours. Jordin erupted out of the exit doors onto the second floor. The girl flew down the second level of stairs from the landing as the exit door swung closed and smacked her. She fluttered backwards as she flipped onto the steps on her side. She quickly sprung onto all fours, growled loudly in irritation, stood on her two feet, and ripped out of the door.

Jordin ran through the second floor banging on doors, "Help...Please help me! Someone help me please!" She heard a few doors slam shut ahead of her. Several people beat on their dorm room doors shouting because they could not open the doors. The girl continued in pursuit of Jordin. Jordin continuously glanced back as the girl gained on her. As fast as she was capable of making her legs move with her injury, she galloped down the long stretch of the "L" shaped hallway towards the elevator.

Jordin breathed heavy and fast temporarily forgetting her training. Her heart seemed to flutter as sweat dripped from the tip of her nose and brow. The lights flickered continuously and sounds like animal growls were all that held her attention, the sounds got closer and closer, more and more audible. Hairs all over her body stood erect. Tears swelled as Jordin's hazel eyes moved frantically. *I'm stuck.* She realized she had no way out; no escape from this insane, inhumane woman. She couldn't make it down another flight of stairs.

Jordin turned the corner of the "L" shaped hallway onto the shorter hallway so quickly she broke her heel, twisted her ankle, fell, and slid against the wall. The pain rippled through her body like a shockwave. "Aaaaagh!" She wailed. The adrenaline dump caused her to ignore the pain and immediately stand. She ran with a serious limp towards the elevator. The girl turned the corner behind her gaining on her quickly; eight feet…, seven feet…, six feet…, and closing. The elevator dinged. Jordin made it her business to catch it at all costs.

Michael stepped out of the elevator as she approached. She gasped. She attempted to stop so she could turn and run the other way. Panicking, and not being rational, her first thought was to run away from Michael without considering she was running towards the inhumane girl, but placed too much weight on her twisted ankle, stumbled to the floor on her side, and slid into the wall. Michael stepped around Jordin as she slid into the wall. The girl continued to run after Jordin despite Michael's presence. After smacking the wall, Jordin crawled to the elevator. She reached her arm out sticking her hand in between the doors before they completely closed. The doors opened. She crawled into the elevator. The doors closed then took her down.

CHAPTER TWO

Beliah sat in a chair near the edge of the trench. The dark red hue of the lava lake slowly flowed with a diffuse glow as he somberly glanced up through the opening at the purple and blue sky during sunrise. Across from him rested the sharp, ragged wall of the volcano with the lava lake between them. The thick slow moving lava had light spots similar to sun spots as it spilled over like it spewed down a decline as with water flowing down a tiny waterfall. The volcano was the only place he felt he could be alone and away from the other fallen angels, nephilim, and lost souls of mankind.

Beliah wished he had gone with his gut feeling. Something just wasn't right about The Adversary's plan. Something didn't feel right about his impending kingdom although the idea of it was most appealing because Beliah did not desire to bow down to humans. He had no respect for beings made of dust while the angels were made with fire. It didn't make sense to him for The Father to give humans a kingdom. It didn't make sense to him for the lesser to rise above the greater.

Beliah did not desire to fight his own brothers. He did not desire to hurt anyone. He only desired to be free. He desired to live on his terms and not have to worry about sin. He did not want to serve. He wanted to be of his own but not in the manner in which The Adversary desired. Beliah did not want to be like the Most High. He did not want to be worshipped or praised. He did not desire glory. He wanted his own territory away from the second heaven. He desired a planet of his own, Jupiter, within the sphere of the first heaven. He desired a wife. He felt, if humans could have a wife, why couldn't he? He lusted for human women and took himself a wife from the descendants of Cain. He thought if he joined the rebellion, The Father would give him Jupiter, let him keep his wife, and let him keep his son. Instead, his son was killed and he faced eternal punishment.

As he sat, The Adversary ran his fingers across his broad muscular shoulder. Beliah peered up as The Adversary coyly walked from behind him to in front of him. Beliah looked away from The Adversary in disgust as he clenched his large hands together. The Adversary said, "Brother, you do not appear enthused to see me. I have not seen you in over three millenniums. Why is that?"

Beliah's dark brown eyes, so dark they almost appeared black, pierced through The Adversary as his thick red eyebrows frowned, "You tell me?"

The Adversary crossed his muscular arms and stroked his blonde beard, so blonde it almost appeared white, with his index finger and thumb, "I prefer your version of the story as opposed to mine."

Beliah stood, at almost 9 feet tall, dusted his hands off by rubbing them together then said, "My hands are clean."

The Adversary, almost a foot shorter but around 150 pounds heavier than Beliah, looked up at Beliah and said, "Are they? How quickly do we forget?"

While walking away from The Adversary in the opposite direction of the stream of lava, "You do not have my allegiance. I suggest you see yourself out."

As he slowly followed Beliah, "Siding with them? You actually think you can earn your way back into the heavens? You think you can earn His love? Stop wasting your time and effort. It's futile."

"I don't care for your words or your opinions. My fate is sealed and so is yours. You should take your own advice. Stop wasting your time and effort. It's futile."

"Beliah, displeased as usual. You followed me on your own freewill. You were my biggest supporter helping me persuade the others. If this was not your desire, you should have listened to your own conscience. Blame yourself for the choices you made."

Beliah turned then walked into The Adversary's face as his eyebrows grimaced, his deep voice with the sound of a bass drum said,

"Cunning, slick, and sly. I can't wait to watch you burn."

The Adversary snarled, "You will be right there with me, brother."

"As long as I get the pleasure of watching you fall and hearing you scream, it is more than worth the penalty...brother."

The Adversary grabbed Beliah by his shoulders and slammed him to the ground. As Beliah's back smacked the ground, the ground rumbled as rocks sprinkled down from the opening of the volcano. The Adversary growled as saliva dribbled from his mouth and his fangs grew long, "I could kill you."

As he lain on the ground without trying to get up, "You won't. You need me as much as I need you."

"I'm listening."

Beliah sat up with one leg straight and the other leg bent as he leaned against his knee, "I can get close to Michael. Can you?"

The Adversary reached his hand out for Beliah to grab. Beliah stared at his big strong hand then grabbed a hold of it. The Adversary yanked Beliah to his feet, "Now whose cunning, slick, and sly?"

"No trickery. I help you. You help me."

"What is it you desire?"

"I want a meeting with the Father."

The Adversary laughed, "Cannot be serious."

"I'm serious. Get me a meeting, and I will keep Michael busy. I can keep him far away from her."

The Adversary rubbed his chin with his thumb and index finger. He slowly walked around Beliah in a circle as the tiny bit of light reflecting off the lava cast a shadow on his left side, "You despise me, yes?"

"I despise him more."

The Adversary smirked, "You hate all around the board. Like that. Close to loving that. I'll allow you to live for the time being." He stepped into Beliah's face almost nose to nose. "Do not get any ideas. You cannot hide from me and you are no match for me."

Beliah smirked, "Understood."

The Adversary stepped back and stared at Beliah, "You are up to something, interesting, nonetheless." The Adversary walked away. Beliah kept his eyes on him. The Adversary stopped and said, "You will get your meeting after you do your part."

CHAPTER THREE

Sonya nestled in her bed like a newborn baby in her mother's arms. Her long medium brown hair like silk spread wildly across her pillow as her face was sandwiched between the mattress and her comforter. Sonya gripped the pillow tightly with her hands, turning her head slowly back and forth every minute or so then remained immobilized for a spell. She released her tight grip succumbing to the manifestations of her dreams. She tossed and turned, tossed and turned, moaned and sighed, moaned and sighed, ferociously battling the fantasies of her mind; her continued sleep pattern.

The sound of a rattle snakes tail rattling awakened her from her slumber. She sat up in the bed as her eyes attempted to focus through the darkness of the room; hands tightly clinched the comforter she held near her mouth. A streak of light from the moon shone through a crack in her thick maroon curtains in the stillness of the room slightly illuminating the closet door. She heard a snake's rattle again as she pierced the bedroom door with her eyes. In order to run out of the room, she had to go passed the closet door. She heard a snake's rattle again but couldn't make out its location although the sound seemed to come from the closet.

A shoe fell over in the closet making a hollow clucking sound as she directed her attention towards the closet door which was slightly cracked. The hairs on the back of her neck stood erect and she felt a horrible presence that made her heart beat fast. She knew *someone was there but could not see them. She slowly, quietly crawled out of her queen-sized bed as her bare feet gripped the cold tile floor in procession to exit her room. Her closet door slowly crept open stopping her in her tracks. The hinges creaked through the silence. The Adversary stepped out from behind the closet door.*

Sonya's eyes and mouth opened wide as she stared at him frozen. He stood with hypnotizing almond shaped sapphire blue eyes. His build typical of a heavy weight boxer and his smile — the beauty of it was a word yet to be defined. His smooth deep voice said, "Do not be afraid."

Sonya stood cemented to the floor as thoughts filled her mind but could not be put into words. The Adversary smirked, "Michael." He pointed towards Sonya's bedroom window as the curtains flew open. She turned and peered out. Michael stood watching her with a blank expression on his face. He opened his mouth revealing fangs then he roared as the sound of the roar echoed.

Sonya awakened, heart racing as the dorm room lights reflected the dampness of her skin. She wiped her eyes with the palms of her hands allowing her vision to slowly focus. She examined the dorm room with her eyes immediately piercing the clock. It read 12:29 a.m. in hazy red digits. She swam through her light blue satin sheets stretching and yawning as the sound of the keyboard keys quickly tapping filled the silence then ceased. A number two pencil landed on her boob unsharpened and unused. Sonya picked up the pencil and tossed it across the room at her roommate then sat up.

"Ha! You missed." Jordin teased as she sat at her light oak wooden desk typing on her laptop like a mad scientist working on her most ingenious plan, "Another one?"

Sonya pulled the strap of her soft pink spaghetti strapped night shirt onto her shoulder and ironed her shirt with her hands. She rubbed her forehead, gently up and down with her palms. She sighed, "Yeah."

Jordin ceased typing and peered around her laptop, "The devil again?"

"Yep, but also about the guy that's been following you. His name is Michael."

Sonya scooted to the edge of the bed and placed her bare feet on the tan tiled floor; cold as usual. She sighed and rubbed her nose with the palm of her hand. Sonya combed her hair with her fingers, pulling her hair behind her shoulders but some of her thick wavy hair fell over the front of her golden shoulders. She sighed.

Jordin cut her eyes sharply towards Sonya's direction, "Michael hunh?"

"Yep."

Jordin shut down her laptop, "It was only a silly dream. His name could be anything."

"It wasn't a dream. It had to be a vision. These dreams are so real like when I was little…and saw energies."

"Energies? What?" Jordin's dark brown arched eyebrows crumbled.

"The silhouettes of dead spirits. They'd be there one second then gone the next. I had terrible dreams that didn't make any sense, but haven't had any since I was 12 until now."

Jordin smirked. Sonya stood up, slid her feet into her light pink furry slippers that had a permanent home next to her bed. She grabbed her dream dictionary from the wall mounted two shelf walnut wooden bookcase that hovered over the end of her bed. She sat at her light oak wooden desk that rested directly across from Jordin's desk.

Sonya said, "Funny? Was it funny when that woman chased you down the hall?"

"All I know is something ain't right. Ever since you've been studying the bible, you've been having these eccentric nightmares. How many nights a week do you wake up out your sleep afraid to go back to sleep? Too many if you ask me," Jordin stood then walked to her closet searching for a jacket to wear.

Jordin pulled a black, waist-length, thin, suede jacket from the closet, put it on then adjusted the collar to fit comfortably around her neck. She slipped her yellow ponytail holder off as her mid-back length dark brown hair trickled down. She tossed the ponytail holder onto her dresser, looked into the mirror that hung above her dresser on the wall then grabbed her brush. She brushed her hair and fluffed it out with her hands then buttoned her jacket.

Sonya opened her dream dictionary and flipped through it. She said, "I don't understand why you refuse to believe after what happened to you."

"The drinks were laced with PCP, okay? I was trippin'," Jordin said as she slid her sterling silver and Amethyst earrings into her ears.

"Tripping...Right. You ran for your life and twisted your ankle for a man and a woman who was a figment of your hallucination...I don't believe that. I know for a fact the effects of PCP. The small dose that would have been in your drink last for 6 to 12 hours and are noticeable between 30 to 90 minutes after ingestion. Nice try."

"Then don't believe me then. Simply because you don't believe something doesn't make it more or less true. I was under the influence."

"You need to take your own advice on that one...What about that man? You saw him days before that happened. Every time you see him, strange things happen. Were you hallucinating every time?"

Jordin smirked, "Look at me." She modeled herself, "Who wouldn't want this? Besides, I'm not worried about him. I have a knife and mace."

"You need an exorcist."

Jordin raised her left eyebrow, "You've got jokes."

"Where are you going?"

"None of your business mom."

"Don't get chased again."

"Don't have any more nightmares." Jordin said as she grabbed her purse then exited the dorm room.

CHAPTER FOUR

Pastor Jones stood at the altar in his small 50 member, 150 person capacity church; a tall 6 feet 3 inch handsome man with a Mediterranean complexion and athletic build in his early thirties. His chiseled body could be seen through his black long sleeve button down dress shirt. He scratched the back of his head as his sandy brown ponytail wiggled in response to the deep scratching.

He rehearsed his sermon; dryly without any emotion, "In life, we have freewill so we must be careful about the choices we make. Our choices not only impact our lives here on this earth, they also impact our destiny."

Pastor Jones stopped and sighed in dissatisfaction. He picked the black ink pen up from the podium and scratched out three lines of his sermon. He tried to prepare a sermon for the past two days but the right words would not formulate in his head.

His sermons sounded staged and poorly dramatized. He was normally, enthusiastic, charming, and eloquent in his speech. He had the flare and charisma to make anyone shout "Amen" without just cause. Members wondered if he was ill or under a lot of stress because his enthusiasm, charm, and eloquence had died.

Thunder roared abruptly. Pastor Jones dropped his pen, heart rate accelerated, and his eyes widened. The lights in the church flickered then dimmed. Pastor Jones' deep blue topaz colored eyes examined the ceiling lights with a hint of concern as he glanced around the church. No one was there.

An angry dog's growl echoed the silence as his hand trembled slightly causing his complexion to turn pale as his eyes wandered quickly. He stood frozen while peering around the church for a few seconds; no one in sight. He cleared his throat and loosened the neck of his tie as he journeyed towards the rows of seating on the floor. His black snake-skinned flats glided across the hairless carpet as he paced towards the front of the church grabbing the doorknob, turning it; locked.

He rubbed his close shaved beard. *I'm scaring myself.* He chuckled as he proceeded towards the podium.

Behind the podium, he continued his rehearsal, dryly, "We are both of flesh and spirit. When our physical body dies, we live in the spirit. This spirit we have is not eternal and can be destroyed. But we have the freedom to choose. We can choose to save our souls by giving our lives…"

"Give your allegiance to me. That would be the wisest," The Adversary rudely interrupted Pastor Jones.

Pastor Jones tensely observed the church with his eyes as he tightly gripped his notebook with his strong wide hands, but didn't see anyone; fear rising.

He nervously questioned, "Who…whose there?"

The Adversary appeared before him; eight feet tall, embodied in a captivating brilliant light with a light canary yellow hue. Pastor Jones' eyes opened wide in dismay and disbelief; speechless and motionless. The Adversary walked toward him smiling. His smile was the most gorgeous, picturesque, and enchanting smile Pastor Jones had ever witnessed. It was so mesmerizing Pastor Jones almost knelt to him.

The Adversary said, "Don't be afraid little Billy. I will not hurt you. I am here to talk business."

Pastor Jones' hands danced uncontrollably as his eyes quivered, "Who are you?" He abruptly questioned.

"I am the one who was, but is not and is yet to come." The Adversary arrogantly boasted.

All of the color drained out of Pastor Jones' face, "Couldn't be. Demons are…"

"Hideous, beastly, monstrosities?" The Adversary smirked as he drew near Pastor Jones; his voice smooth, smoky, and eloquent. "I love your kind. In the art gallery of your mind, hang images of me that as you can see, are false. Second Commandment Pastor; do not make any graven images of anything in heaven above or on the earth or in the waters below. I must say your gruesome mental depictions insult me." He batted his eyes and smirked. "I am the most beautiful angel; once loved above all."

Pastor Jones stood frozen as he slowly blinked continuously wiping his eyes. He told himself it wasn't real; he's simply overworked, overtired, and hallucinating. His vision blurred regaining focus.

The Adversary posed, reminiscent of a statue of Buddha, hovered before Pastor Jones in Indian style. He stared at Pastor Jones transferring his thoughts into his head, "I know your desires, Billy. You used to dream of one day becoming a Pope until the lust of your flesh got the best of you. I can ensure you will be Pope if you follow me. You and I have much in common. I can make you the most powerful man in the world."

Pastor Jones grabbed his head, pulled his hair, and clenched his teeth, "Make it stop. Please."

The Adversary ignored his request and continued staring him deeply into his eyes.

Pastor Jones smacked himself in the head as his veins dilated, "What are you doing to me?...Stop...Stop."

He hysterically walked around in a stagnated circle as impressions of someone choking him appeared on his neck. Pastor Jones continuously grabbed his neck in an attempt to remove the invisible force because the veins in his hands swelled as his eyes bulged. He desperately pulled at the collar of his shirt.

The Adversary released him from the trance of possession.

Pastor Jones turned towards the podium gasping for air as he continuously coughed and rubbed his chest.

He hugged the podium hoping the gold painted crucifix would offer him some kind of protection. He screamed, "Why me?"

"Why not you? Your sins elude you. You enjoy the pleasures of your flesh keeping multitudes of women in your bed behind your wife's back. You hide your treachery well. Impressive in the manner at which you hide behind the cloth. You're certainly my kind of guy."

Pastor Jones slowly stepped away from The Adversary, "So what do you want from me?"

The Adversary hovered closer to Pastor Jones, "Your body; temporarily of course."

Pastor Jones stood rigidly exposing the raised hairs on the back of his neck, "My body?... Why me? Why a man of God?"

"You are so far from God he is nothing more than a meaningless word to you. How does it feel Pastor? You preach words every

Sunday that you do not mean nor believe in for that matter. You are a minister because you love power, money, and influence not because you love God," The Adversary stood next to Pastor Jones. "We have more in common than you may imagine. Good looking, charming, cunning, influential, insatiable thirst for power and authority; you and I. Who better to represent my motives in the flesh... momentarily?"

"You know nothing about me," Pastor Jones said as his voice quivered and he walked beside the podium; a clear path to the front door.

"I know you better than you know yourself. After all, I am the god of this world. Multitudes upon multitudes freely give their allegiance to me. Your congregation already has my mark."

Pastor Jones attempted to run away by stepping down from the altar to head down the middle aisle. The Adversary immobilized him with a gaze stopping him in his tracks. Pastor Jones tried to run, but could not move a muscle; not even in his face.

After a few seconds, The Adversary released him; toying with him. Pastor Jones tried to run again, but no matter what he tried, he could not run or walk further than the boundary of an invisible three feet square.

Pastor Jones said, "This is a church of God. I rebuke you Satan. I rebuke you in the name of Jesus Christ."

"He doesn't know you Pastor. Not everyone who says to him, Lord, Lord, will enter the kingdom of heaven, but only he who does the will of his Father, which you do not."

Pastor Jones' face turned red as he clinched his fists and his muscles tensed; flexing through his button down shirt, "You are the prince of lies. You lie. All lies. I am a child of God."

"Sorry but you're not. You are a child of mine, you and the majority of the automatons in this world. You want to do your own will instead of his, and frankly, I don't blame you. Make no mistake young Billy. You belong to me and always have. You enjoy the freedom I bestow upon you."

"What if I don't give you my body?" Pastor Jones' shoulders slumped as his eyes narrowed.

The Adversary responded, "Frankly, you don't have a choice. This is not a foray. You *will* be the next Pope and you *will* thank me later. It's not like it's the first time Billy…memory lapses?…awakening in a woman's bed not knowing how you got there?"

Pastor Jones had a stunned expression on his face. The Adversary slid into Pastor Jones' nostrils as smoke being inhaled. Once in

Pastor Jones' body, he cracked his neck, fixed his collar, and ironed his shirt with his hands.

He walked to a framed poster of Jesus on the wall and stared at it. "These humans have no idea how far off their depictions are; blue eyes?" He giggled to himself.

He admired his reflection in the glass turning his head side to side. He slid the ponytail holder off, tossed it on the floor, and allowed his shoulder length, shiny hair to flow naturally. He licked his fingers and slicked his hair in its proper place, combing it with his fingers. He turned his head side to side again examining his profile. He smiled, licked his lips, and rubbed his close shaved beard with his thumb and fingers cuffed in front of his face. "Shall I begin?"

CHAPTER FIVE

The dark stillness of nightfall was both peaceful and calm. The bitter cold temperature of late autumn felt like winter as the gusty wind molested Jordin's body, caressed her face, and played with her hair. The dog's bark echoed in the distance as the crescent moon shined against the dark sky. As she peered up, she noticed the sky wasn't as dark as other nights as the stars sprinkled across the sky appeared to wink at her. Had she paid attention in high school, she could point out the constellations, but all that was on her mind was remaining eligible to run track.

Every step she took was slow and painful. Her limp was worse than before. Overnight, the pain in her right hip marinated, bruised perhaps but could not be broken. Her swollen ankle suffocated in her high heel boots, so she decided to change. Sneakered tonight, the laces of her white ankle cut shoes were laced loose around her right ankle.

Arms folded across her chest, she held herself battling the wind feeling every degree of the cold. Cars rode by some played music loudly while others were silent except for engine sounds. The air smelled fresh as a group of guys walked passed her coming from the sorority party. The scent of their different fragrances welcomed a lingering stare. One guy smiled at her while the others were busy laughing. She remembered when she could laugh.

A peculiar feeling struck the core of her soul. She turned around quickly searching behind her, across the street, and ahead of her. She felt someone watching her. The wind blew the plaid cotton hat off of her head. It tumbled and slid six feet behind her. She chased her hat as it blew, hobbling. She grabbed it and held it in her hands tightly. She looked around again.

The baggage under her eyes revealed many sleepless nights that she blamed on Sonya's mid-night awakening episodes. She didn't understand what was happening. She didn't know who or what haunted her. She only knew she was haunted or perhaps cursed.

She yearned to call her mother and tell her, but as a clinical psychologist, Jordin doubted her mother would do more than commit her. Sonya? Enlightening her on the terror that resided in her soul would be useless. If she was afraid, Sonya would become afraid. How would anyone be able to sleep if Sonya became more and more afraid of her dreams? Some things were simply better left unsaid.

The dance music became more and more audible as Jordin approached the sorority house. She wasn't in the mood to party, but she needed to find Ayana. Ayana was the only person who could rationalize the strange occurrences without any biases. Jordin desired more than a simple 'pray about it'. She needed some answers.

Two houses away and the music was almost deafening for Jordin's keen sense of hearing. A handful of people lounged outside, mostly on the porch with a few standing in the yard. Upon the sight of her friend Ayana, Jordin smiled enthusiastically. Ayana staggered towards her in bright orange six inch stilettos while stroking her short, crisply styled jet black hair ensuring nothing was out of place. Ayana hugged Jordin careful not to spill or drop her drink. Jordin embraced her tightly as though she did not want to ever let her go.

"Hey lady!...I can't breathe." Ayana blurted in the thick Jamaican accent she desperately tried to hide.

"Sorry." Jordin released her. "I have never been so damn happy to see you."

Ayana took a sip of her drink then stared at Jordin's shoes. "Nike's?" She frowned. "I haven't seen ya in sneakers since high school. Are ya okay?"

Jordin paused and shook her head "no". Ayana placed her arm around her shoulder as they walked towards the sorority party. "When ya wear sneakers, we're the same height, ya know?"

Jordin snickered, "Only because your heels are so high. There aren't too many women walking around here that's 5'11"."

The weight of Ayana's athletic frame and thoroughbred legs sent a shock of pain from Jordin's hip to her ankle. Jordin stumbled a little causing Ayana to stumble with her spilling some of her drink. Jordin said, "I'm sorry."

Ayana removed her hand from across Jordin's shoulder. "It's okay…So why are ya in sneakers, diva?"

Jordin tried to hide her limp as they walked. "I hurt my ankle and hip."

Ayana stared at Jordin's leg. "Mmm. Ya get that checked out?"

"No."

Ayana smacked her lips together, "Was it Roger? Has he hit ya again?"

"No. No. He didn't do this. We've been over. I don't talk to him or see him."

"Can't say I'm not happy to hear that. Ya better be glad this isn't track season. Can't afford to lose your scholarship again. What happened?"

Jordin exhaled slowly with a blank expression on her face as they entered the yard. "I don't even know where to begin. Do you believe in ghosts, demons, and shit like that?"

Ayana placed her foot on the bottom step. The music pounded with vibrations that could be felt as well as heard. The beat seemed to penetrate Jordin's body to the point she could no longer feel her own heartbeat just the rhythm of the music. Ayana leaned towards Jordin. "No. I believe in good spirits and evil spirits. For everything good there is something bad. All things have to balance themselves out. If there is a holy trinity, there is also an unholy trinity. If angels exist then so do demons if that's what you believe. For me, there are no angels and demons. Evil spirits are nothing more than lost human souls."

Jordin glanced at the porch looking through the screen door. Her thirst got the best of her. "Is there any more of what you're drinking?"

"Sure is. Follow me."

CHAPTER SIX

Ayana grabbed a red plastic cup from the stack of cups on the kitchen table. The green plastic table cloth stuck to her form fitting imitation denim jeans like static. She pulled the table cloth away revealing an ice cream stain. She grabbed a napkin and wiped the ice cream only smearing it into a larger stain. She shook her head in disapproval as she poured Jordin two scoops of red punch with the vanilla and strawberry ice cream floating on top. She handed it to Jordin.

Jordin glared out of the double pane kitchen window with the feeling that someone was watching her. The thick bushes and trees illuminated on the left side from the moonlight. There was nothing except darkness.

Jordin took a sip of her drink. She coughed. "This is strong."

"Ya think? I can barely stand." Ayana ingested the last drop of her drink then tossed the cup into the thirteen gallon trash can. She ironed her shirt with her hands. Jordin picked a piece of lent out of Ayana's hair as she walked by and tossed it.

A man with emerald green eyes and dark brown hair walked near the kitchen on his way to the living room coming from the bathroom. Ayana playfully tapped Jordin on her shoulder and said, "Watch and learn my friend."

Jordin grabbed Ayana's arm stopping her, "Can I show you something?"

Ayana said, "Sure."

Jordin lead her into the bathroom.

Once in the bathroom, Jordin closed and locked the door. Ayana leaned against the glass shower door. Jordin said, "Can you keep a secret?"

"Of course I can."

"You have to promise me," Jordin asserted.

Ayana cross her fingers, "I promise on my mother's life."

Jordin set her drink on the marble top sink, lifted up her shirt, and turned her back to Ayana revealing three large bite marks, four inches long and two inches wide. Ayana's eyes bulged as she touched one of the bites.

Jordin shuddered, "Don't touch it."

"What the hell happen to ya?" Ayana questioned.

Jordin pulled her shirt down and turned to Ayana. "I don't know. I felt pain in my sleep. I woke up, looked in the mirror, and saw these bites. Stuff like this only seems to happen when I'm around Sonya,"

"It seems ya been picked."

"What do you mean…picked?"

"Ya been chosen by an evil spirit."

"What? How do you know this?" Jordin picked up her drink.

"I just do."

"Why?"

"That is something I don't know."

"What can I do about it?"

"For starters finish ya drink and enjoy this party. Then find ya a witch doctor. Only a witch doctor can unmark ya." Ayana unlocked the bathroom door, opened it, and walked out.

Jordin followed her.

As they walked towards the living room, Jordin asked, "Where do I find one?"

"Online. Google search."

"Google?"

"I don't know any witch doctors." Ayana walked outside on the porch. Jordan followed her.

"You're afraid of me aren't you?"

Ayana stopped and turned to Jordin, "It's not you I fear. I don't know what kind of spirit has marked ya. From the look of things, ya may have a class 5 or 6 spirit. There are specific reasons spirits choose people, too many to name right now. The spirit that has chosen ya can and will attack the people ya around." Ayana walked down the steps.

Jordan followed. She grabbed Ayana's arm to stop her, "Why?"

"To isolate you."

Jordin scratched her head, "I don't understand."

"Get ya some salt and place it in ya pockets. Keep a mirror with ya at all times. When something happens flash the mirror at it. These things wards off evil spirits."

"That's it. What else can be done?"

"I will have to ask my grandmother." Ayana walked towards the end of the yard.

Jordin limped behind her, "This man. This man has been following me. Every time he shows up things happen."

As she walked down the street towards her car, "Then it's him. He's the spirit who's chosen ya."

Tears filled Jordin's eyes, "What about Sonya?"

"What about her?"

"She's been having nightmares again seems like ever since that man started followin' me."

"Ya have a serious problem then. That spirit could kill her." Ayana exhaled. "I wish there was a way to help ya, but once chosen, the spirit will not stop until it destroys ya."

Jordin placed her hands around her mouth and bit down on her bottom lip. She blinked rapidly to prevent her tears from falling, "Why would a spirit want to destroy me?"

"I don't know. The best I can do for ya is to call my grandmother. Maybe she will have some answers."

"What do I do in the meantime?"

"Pray."

CHAPTER SEVEN

Sonya sat at her desk searching her dream dictionary for the meaning of wind in a dream as she listened to the radio; slow songs relaxed her. She was awakened from her sleep because she had an extremely frightening dream; similar to the one she had the previous night. She flipped through the letter "W" section fingering down the words; wilderness, willow, wilted, win, all the way to the word wind. According to the dictionary, the wind had several meanings. Blowing wind in a dream symbolized life force, energy, vigor, and changes in life. Gusty or violent winds symbolized turmoil and trouble in life. From a religious aspect, it was symbolic of the Holy Spirit's outpouring among believers. Sonya closed her eyes as she recalled her dream:

Sonya stood in the middle of a dirt road surrounded by seven feet tall thick bushes. The road was bright sinking into the horizon in front of her. Behind her, the road was pitch black swallowing the horizon. Above her, the sky was peppered with shades of dark green, fuchsia, light pink, red, bright yellow, light & dark blue, and purple; reminiscent of an abstract painting, that consistently changed within an invisible vortex. A strong wind blew violently bending the bushes, but didn't move one strand of her hair.

The ground rumbled under her feet as she heard a loud explosion. Behind her, the darker sky disclosed a portal. As the portal opened, a multitude of dark creatures on pale horses armed for battle ran towards the ground. She heard a loud trumpet in front of her. The brighter sky revealed a portal. A multitude of beautiful illuminated creatures on white horses armed for battle ran towards the ground as the portal opened.

Both armies ran towards her, but she was frozen, immobile; cemented. The armies closed in on both sides; fear arisen in Sonya. Her panicky head turned back and forth as she noticed the swiftness of the approaching armies. The leaders of both armies closed in, with Sonya stuck in the middle they drew their swords and swung.

Sonya opened her eyes panting as sweat glistened on her forehead. She rubbed her eyes with the palms of her hands as her hands trembled. She stretched out her arms and watched her hands dance uncontrollably as she inhaled and exhaled slowly. *That's too real. I don't care what anybody says. This isn't an ordinary dream.* She reread the sentence and reflected on the fact the wind did not affect nor touch her. She couldn't make a correlation but desired an answer. She closed the dream dictionary and picked up her bible. She opened the back cover where a handwritten name and phone number was located, picked up the phone, and dialed the phone number.

Pastor Jones sat in his office at his desk, tossing a gold coin into the air and singing. The phone rang twice. He answered it, "Hello!"

Sonya said, "Pastor, its Sonya. Remember me?"

Pastor Jones leaned back in his chair and placed his feet on top of his desk, "Aw yes. Faithful and true. I remember you. How have you been? It's been a while since we spoke."

"You tell me. Lately, I've been having these strange dreams that don't make any sense," Sonya mentioned as she twirled her hair afraid to disclose the depth of her dreams.

Pastor Jones placed the phone on his shoulder and grabbed a snow globe from his desk, shook it, and giggled, "Well, all dreams are strange; a meaningless collage of memories and ideas."

"That's not what I meant to say because these dreams aren't memories. They're things I've never seen before. I've been dreaming about endless wars with me caught in the middle. It's like a war between good and evil but both sides are attacking me. It's just so hard to explain right now…I'm so tired; haven't been sleeping well."

Pastor Jones sat the snow globe down on his desk and leaned back, "Your dreams are nothing more than a manifestation of your own guilt. They're expressing an internal conflict; a warning from above. You seem to be caught in the middle of what is righteous and the road that leads to destruction. I'm afraid to tell you, but Pastor Ryan is not a true man of God. He is leading you and his congregation astray. You have to make a choice. Are you going to live in righteousness? Or are you going to continue walking in utter darkness?"

"What?" Sonya softly inquired.

Pastor Jones continued, "Pastor Ryan is not spiritually mature and doubts the same teachings he allows you to believe in. Trust me, I know. He was my professor at the seminary several years ago. He is feeding you milk instead of the solid food of the Word. I can ensure you are fed the meat of the word so you have the knowledge and wisdom to prevent yourself from deception. The sooner you leave his congregation the sooner your dreams will end."

"They will?... How can you be so sure?" Sonya squinted her small slanted eyes as her eye brows crumbled.

"Have a little faith. Do you trust me?"

"Yeah. Of course I...."

Pastor Jones interrupted, "Then act like it. Watch out for false prophets. They come to you in sheep's clothing, but inwardly they are ferocious wolves. I'm not telling you this to hurt you; let's make sure we're one on that. Sometimes, the truth hurts especially when we find out all we ever believed to be true is a lie. I tell you this because I care about helping you save your soul from eternal damnation. You will be so much better off a member of my congregation. Why don't you visit my church to see for yourself?"

"I…I… I'll consider it Pastor. It certainly sounds like you know exactly what you're talking about. I certainly will think about it."

"You do just that, but do not wait too long. The day and the hour are unknown so time is of the essence," Pastor Jones reminded.

"Thank you Pastor. I will speak with you later."

"Sweet dreams Sonya. You take care of yourself and have a good night."

Pastor Jones hung up the phone, "And even I have been transformed into an angel of light." He shook his head in disapproval then turned toward the dark corner of the room, "What is it you need?"

Jaie appeared beyond the dark corner of the room near the window as a dark humanoid silhouette, "He is here."

Pastor Jones leisurely strode towards Jaie emotionlessly, "Really? As if I didn't already know that." Pastor Jones stared out of the window, unbuttoning the first two buttons of his white dress shirt. He rubbed the sweat from his neck with his hand as he thought aloud, mumbling, "What is your purpose?"

"What should we do?" Jaie inquired.

Pastor Jones paused, slowly inhaled then exhaled, "Nothing. Nothing at all. He's no threat.

"How can you be so sure?"

Pastor Jones stared at the bible on his desk, "Trust me... Once you find her, fill me in. I'll handle everything from there."

Jaie inquired, "Is that all?"

Pastor Jones checked the time on his gold Rolex. It read 2:20 a.m., "Find out what he wants; the reason he is here."

"Of course."

"That will be all."

Jaie turned and before long vanished.

Pastor Jones rubbed the fog from the cold window and wiped his moist hand onto his black slacks. His eyes narrowed as he focused to see through the darkness of the early morning, placing his forearm on the window above his head, as he leaned his forehead against his forearm. His breath steamed the window as his eyebrows collapsed expressing his uneasiness. He thought back to the last time he saw Michael face to face.

INTERLUDE

Lucifer returned to the ledge in Midst to address his legions of Sons of God, "Prepare for battle. The Father has banished us from the heavens, but we aren't going anywhere. This is our time to prove who we are and what we stand for." The Sons of God stood in silent bewilderment speculating what happened. Some Sons of God stood distressingly at the shattered dream of having their own kingdom.

Beliah joined Lucifer on the ledge and inquired, "Why have we been banished?"

Lucifer gazed upon him in the deepest, darkest sarcasm, "Because those humans sinned. I have been blamed for their fallibility. Contrary to what many believe, The Father is not just and true. We have served him for millenniums upon millenniums and have been complacent and obedient. It is time for us to rise up against this injustice. Are you with me?"

Beliah stared at Lucifer in silence as he mentally straddled the fence on what action he should take; which side he should be on as doubts about Lucifer flooded his mind. The Sons of God stood in silence contemplating if they had made a mistake in following Lucifer in response to Beliah's lack of reaction to his question. Besides Baal and Molech, Beliah was Lucifer's principal advocate and co-conspirator in persuading them to follow him in the first place.

Zoez stepped up and shouted, "I am with you." He turned to face the others and said, "Don't tell me you are jumping ship when we've come so far. From Lucifer's own mouth, we were promised a kingdom as The Father has reneged. We must fight for what is rightfully ours. How much longer do you want to be servants? How much longer should we have to submit to senseless demands? We were given freewill. It is passed due for us to exercise this marvelous gift. Shall we live our eternity in chains? No! I say no! Now is the time for us to break free. It is time to let The Father know how we truly feel. Are you with us?"

The Sons of God shouted in unison and clapped rhythmically, "Yeah!"

Zoez turned to Lucifer as he placed his right arm across his chest and slammed his fist against the location of his heart, "We are ready for battle."

Lucifer stood in admiration and gratitude of his legions. He turned to Beliah, "Are you with me brother?" Beliah stared into Lucifer's eyes prepared to deny him regardless of the consequence then stared downward at the Legions observing their delight and fervor, "Of course." Lucifer smiled as he pulled his two bronze swords out of their sling cases; one in each hand. One sword was six feet long and was designed like a machete. The other sword was eight feet long with the tip shaped like a trident. Lucifer held both swords at chest level and turned to Beliah, "Let us prepare but make sure you leave Michael unscathed for he is mine."

Michael stood impatiently and nervously before the legions of guardian angels, with the five archangels beside him, and the transparent golden spear inscribed with the untranslatable language of the Father in his sash on his back. In his right hand, he held a chrome sword with a blade shaped like a flame with three sharp asymmetrical points with a length of seven feet. Michael distressed but attempted to hide the emotion from divulging through his face. He never thought he would ever have to fight one of his own brothers, especially Lucifer. He admired Lucifer and once looked up to him. Within the blink of an eye, Lucifer had become his enemy. Regardless of the hatred that dominated Lucifer, Michael loved him exceedingly and did not want to harm him in any way, shape or form.

Gabriel tapped Michael's shoulder. He turned and peered down as he observed Lucifer and the Sons of God flying into Zion from the second heaven.

Gabriel placed his comforting hand upon Michael's shoulder, "Don't worry brother. You make sure you remain alive. I will dispatch Lucifer."

Michael sighed as he blinked rapidly then closed his eyes and tilted his head down. He lifted his head up as he opened his eyes, "How very considerate and brave of you Gabriel, but I can't allow that. The Father has given me a specific assignment and it must be accomplished."

Gabriel smiled and patted Michael's back like a proud father. Michael, leader of the army of The Father, turned to his angels and said, "Be sure to send as many of them as you can to the abyss. If you can't, cast them down to the earth. Do not allow Lucifer to strike you and do not strike him. Leave him alive for it is my duty and privilege to banish him." Michael turned around and patiently waited for Lucifer and the Sons of God to approach.

The adrenaline in Michael arisen considerably the closer Lucifer and the Sons of God approached. Within a blink, the two armies had collided with one another in an all-out war. Billions upon billions upon billions of angels courageously brawled as The Father, The Son, The elders, the seven spirits of the Father, and others watched from the Holy Mount. The Sons of God were severely outnumbered; two thirds to their one third. Every second Sons of God were thrown into the abyss with most casted to the earth. The Sons of God obeyed Lucifer and ignored Michael as the guardian angels did the same by staying away from Lucifer. Lucifer wasn't concerned with any of the guardians; he wanted Michael and Michael only. He slew the guardian angels that were in his path towards getting to Michael but nothing more.

Michael stood and waited anxiously for Lucifer to come to him. At the sight of Lucifer in the near distance slaying guardians in his path, everything shifted into slow motion to Michael. He inhaled deeply and slowly exhaled as Lucifer drew near. He gripped his sword tightly with both hands as the flame bladed sword blazed like a flame. Lucifer flew in and struck at him with his trident. Lucifer's trident and Michael's sword crashed causing blue sparks at the point of impact. The Sons of God and the guardians and archangels ceased fighting and became the audience of this battle between the two leaders. No one said one word as tensions were enormously high.

Lucifer, struck with the trident then swung with the sword, as Michael's sword clashed the trident knocking it out of the way then collided with Lucifer's sword. This continued for a while until Lucifer became frustrated because he did not expect Michael to be an equally powerful opponent. No matter what they tried neither one of them could pummel the other. Each swing consisted of swords colliding and clashing.

Before Lucifer sinned, he was the most powerful angel. He soon realized, not only did he lose his position in the heavens, he lost his strength. Although he lost the portions of himself that fueled his pride, vanity, and arrogance, he remained a more skillful swordsman than Michael as he stabbed Michael in his right side penetrating diagonally with his sword, tossing his trident to the ground. The guardian angels and archangels gasped and sighed as Lucifer's confidence multiplied.

Michael dropped his sword then grabbed a hold of Lucifer's sword as he endeavored to yank it out of his side. He screamed, "Aaaaaaaagh!"

Lucifer smiled, jostling the sword farther inside of Michael. Michael ceased trying, his head tilted up leaning back as his knees faltered, and he whimpered in fathomless pain. "You should have joined me...brother", Lucifer said as he placed his hand on Michael's shoulder for leverage, screwed the sword, and ripped it out of Michael's side.

It took every scrap of endurance Michael had left in him not to crumble to the ground as he held a portion of his wound with his forearm.

Tears poured from Gabriel's eyes as Uriel almost lifelessly, plummeted to his knees in despair from the agony of Michael's groans.

The Sons of God were awestruck and relieved as they believed at that moment Lucifer was justified and praiseworthy for his self-exaltation.

Beliah thought, *I did the right thing in following him. I should never have doubted.*

Lucifer's eyes morphed into snake eyes as saliva dribbled from his mouth, "Goodbye Michael. It was a pleasure knowing you." Lucifer raised his sword in procession to decapitate Michael.

The Father said, "Utilize your gift, Michael."

Michael remembered the transparent golden spear inscribed with the untranslatable language of the Father in his sash, as his body illuminated radiantly as a means to heal, he quickly pulled the spear out of the sash.

As Lucifer's sword approached a foot from his neck before making contact, Michael struck Lucifer with the spear through his heart. The spear illuminated brilliantly as it absorbed the radiance from Lucifer and expelled the untranslatable language of the Father into him. Once the inscription transferred from the spear into Lucifer's spirit, it became translatable. The words "The Adversary" burned into him as an identifying stamp then dissipated; marking his name change for his iniquity.

Lucifer dropped his sword upon impact of the spear as the razor-sharp blade incised Michael's shoulder; before it bounced and rested on the ground. Lucifer's face exposed his suffering but he refused to scream, shout, or release any sound that disclosed his pain. The power the spear manifested bound Lucifer to the point of rigidity. Tears flooded down Michael's face as he stared into Lucifer's eyes. Lucifer said, "This is... your... moment of ...praise... and glory. Accept... what is... rightfully... yours." Michael replied, "I cannot and I will not. You may have no comprehension of love or obedience, but it is who I am. The Father doesn't desire you lifeless yet. He is showing mercy upon you, so you will live."

Michael spread his wings and flew through Zion from the third heaven on his way down through the heavens of the earth. He traveled with great speed almost as fast as the speed of light with the spear penetrated through Lucifer.

As they approached the earth, Michael yanked the spear out of Lucifer. Once the spear was removed, it disappeared. Michael threw Lucifer in front of him, caught up to him in flight, and carried him by his wings; he remained immobile as the power of the spear continuously flowed through him.

Everyone in the heavens watched intensely as they yearned to find out what Michael planned to do with Lucifer since he refused to kill him.

"Where... are you... taking me?" Lucifer said.

Michael said, "You've corrupted a perfect creation because you desired a kingdom. For a short space, the earth is yours."

Michael hurled Lucifer to the earth as lightning falling from the sky.

The elders on the throne in the Holy Mount of Zion shouted, "Woe to the inhabitants of the earth."

CHAPTER EIGHT

Michael lounged in the corner in the back of Mel's Diner. The smell of cooked food and fresh brewed coffee filled the diner as Michael's mouth watered for a fresh cup of coffee. His thick dark brown eyebrows offered an impression of seriousness as his hairless face revealed his sharp features. His full lips were pinched together, and his close-shaved head rested upon the palm of his large hand. His dark brown eyes revealed his sensitivity.

Michael wasn't much of a looker but was exceptionally clean and neat. Rosa noticed Michael sitting in the corner by himself. She pulled her order booklet out of her pocket and walked towards him. She said, "What can I get for you handsome?" Michael offered her a gorgeous smile; teeth perfectly white, perfectly straight, deep dimples, with soft lips shaped like a cupid's bow. His smile literally lit up the entire room. "I would like a coffee please." She wrote the order down in her order booklet. She asked, "No sugar or cream with that?"

"No ma'am. Thank you."

"Will that be all?" She asked.

"Yes Ma'am", Michael said.

Rosa walked away saying, "It'll be right up."

As Michael waited for his coffee, he stared outside of the window tuning out the sounds within the diner; people talking, forks clinking, the television, etc. He noticed a bum with a sign, standing on the street corner begging for change as traffic sounds were almost shrill. As he watched, every single person walked by without giving him anything. One person, a business man, told him to get a life. Michael was grieved by what he witnessed.

He looked down the street and saw two young men standing in front of an abandoned building selling drugs. He looked up the street and saw a man and a woman walking down the street arguing. The woman appeared to be under a great deal of emotional stress. He looked at the crosswalk and noticed two children walking across the street carrying book bags. They weren't much older than nine or ten years old. A group of five teenage boys walked by and consistently bumped into them without saying, "Excuse me." One teenager walked directly into one of the kids, knocking him down and yelled, "Watch where you going?" as though it was the kid's fault. The teenager's friend's laughed as the little boy laid in a fearful silence. The teenagers continued through the crosswalk while the other little boy helped his friend up. Michael mumbled to himself, *Brother, what have you done?*

Rosa returned to the table with Michael's coffee. She sat it down and placed some napkins on the table. Michael turned to her and said, "Thank you very much." Rosa nodded and walked away. As she walked away, Michael said, "The bill. Ma'am you forgot to give me the bill."

Rosa said, "You're okay. Coffee black, no sugar, no cream, in a four ounce glass is only a dollar early Sunday mornings."

Michael smiled, nodded then took a sip of his coffee almost burning his taste buds as Rosa walked away. He touched his tongue as his finger tip glowed, so he could drink the coffee comfortably without it burning.

A short, Hispanic male sat down across from Michael dressed in baggy jeans, low cut sneakers, a hooded sweatshirt, with a teenage mustache. His head was shaved bald tied with a black scarf. Michael searched around the diner then stared at the young male. The young man, about 18 years old, stared at Michael intently through his dark sunglasses. Michael said, "May I help you?"

The young man said, "It is you."

Michael felt a little uncomfortable, "Do I know you? There must be some kind of mistake. I don't think you know me?"

"I'm Jose."

"Nice to meet you Jose," Michael blew the coffee then took another sip. The deep brewed flavor partied in his mouth.

"Have you fallen?" Jose said loudly and excitedly.

Rosa, the grill cook, the cashier, and the five other people in the diner turned to look at Michael and Jose. Michael choked off of his coffee and motioned Jose to be silent. He momentary looked around at the people offering a smile acknowledging his embarrassment. The people immediately whispered to each other.

Jose in a low, soft tone, "It's okay. Your secret is safe with me. I knew this day would come."

"How do you know who I am?" Michael whispered.

"Word spreads quickly around here."

Michael stared at Jose silently then leaned back in his chair, "Please, remove your glasses."

"Why?"

Michael's eyes shined a bright white light, but no one else could see them except Jose. He grabbed Jose's hands, held them down, binding them to the table as Jose trembled. Michael leaned in, "Nice try."

Beliah, emerged from within Jose as Michael turned Jose's hands loose. Beliah touched Jose's forehead putting him in a temporary deep, conscious sleep. From the point of view of everyone in the diner, Michael appeared to be speaking with Jose. As Beliah sat, Michael said, "What is it you desire?"

"To know why you are here."

"I'm sure the word has spread by now. I'm here on my own accord."

Rosa walked towards Jose and Michael with her order booklet in her hand. She stopped in front of the table and stared at Jose, "May I help you?"

Jose stared directly ahead because he was in a state of deep, conscious sleep. From the point of view of Rosa, he seemed to be blatantly ignoring her.

Michael quickly blurted, "Yes. I would like another coffee please."

Rosa smirked as she wrote his order down, "I knew you'd love my coffee. I make the best in town. How about your friend? Does he want something?"

Michael glanced at Jose then quickly said, "He is fine. He does not desire anything. Thank you."

Rosa stared at Jose for a few seconds, "Alright. Let me know if there's anything else I could get for you." Rosa walked away.

Michael made sure Rosa was a good distance away when he focused his attention on Beliah. Beliah turned to stare at Rosa, and shook his head in disapproval because he could sense she was not a believer.

Beliah turned to Michael, "How is it possible for you to be here on your own accord?"

"The last time I checked Archangels have freewill," Michael took another sip of his coffee.

"Why are you nosing around our kingdom?"

"You call this a kingdom?" Michael slammed his hands down on the table causing the salt and pepper shaker to clink, "I pity you distant brother. You gave up paradise for this? The aroma, aura, and atmosphere of this filth suffocate me. With every glance, glimpse, or sight, my heart breaks repeatedly. The Son created this world and these people perfectly, but you and your brothers, coerced them to poison themselves with sin. Your kind has injected so much wickedness into their hearts, souls, and minds that they despise the ones who created them. This was not the plan for them. Most of these inhabitants are so far gone they deny the truth when in their faces."

Beliah leaned towards Michael, "I've witnessed the Son come down to offer these people a way to break free from the bondage we have placed before them. He allowed himself to be tortured, as a perfect sacrifice to defeat the penalty of sin, so the plan he had for them at creation could still be fulfilled regardless of our corruption, yet they still turn away from him by their own freewill; not by anything we have done."

"It is not enough for you to be banished from the heavens, separated from the Father and his good, glorious, majestic graces, to be cast down here as your prison? Is it?" Michael paused as he quickly glanced out of the window for a few seconds to calm himself down, "Although the Father has done nothing except love you and give you all you desire, you are so intent on hurting him for no reason. How have your hearts grown so cold and dark?" He took another sip of his coffee.

Beliah stared with an expression of irritation and disgust on his face, "You know nothing, Michael. I have been walking this earth for millenniums upon millenniums in the deepest, sunken resentment. My intent was not to hurt the Father. I was deceived in the process. Lucifer, that serpent of old, called The Adversary, loves no one but himself; neither do I. He's looking for a woman whose name is darkness. I suggest you find her before he does."

"I'm not interested in interfering with his will. The Father granted him a short space to rule. He can have darkness as far as I am concerned. I am not here for her. I am here on my own accord. Why do you want me to interfere?" Michael gulped the last swallow of his coffee.

"As I previously stated, I love no one but myself. The Adversary has his plan, and I have one of my own."

"No thank you."

As Beliah was about to speak, Rosa returned with Michael's coffee. She sat it on the table then collected the empty cup.

Michael nodded his head as a means to say, "Thank you."

Rosa stared at Jose because she felt the tension between them. She peered at Michael and said, "Is everything okay?"

Michael said, "All is fine. Thank you for asking."

Rosa stared at Jose with attitude, "Just so you know. Old man Mel keeps a shotgun in back. Don't get any ideas. He will split your cap back. Just letting you know."

Michael smiled and nodded. Rosa walked away. Beliah was irritated with all the interruptions, "Do as you wish, but we will be watching you. You may be obedient Michael, but down here, we play by our own rules. We will find out the reason you are here. Once we do, *he* will interfere." Beliah slid inside of Jose. Jose awakened from his deep sleep.

"If a battle is what you seek, a battle is what you will find. I have no fear of you or your legion. If you interfere with my will, I will personally slay you and your soldiers. While you are at it, bring The Adversary along if you think he will better your chances."

Jose snarled, "I don't desire to be your enemy Michael. How I wish I could turn back the hands of time." He stood.

"Unfortunately, you are my enemy, brother", Michael stated as he somberly turned away from Beliah. He thought back to the first time he heard the phrase "You are my enemy."

INTERLUDE

Lucifer stood on the ledge in the deep valley in Midst before an audience of multitudes of legions of fallen angels, called Sons of Gods, as he peered down at them in deep arrogance. The multitude was exactly one third of the angels in the heavens, once guardian angels that Lucifer cunningly deceived into following him. As Lucifer stood above them, covered in a luxurious bright white robe with a golden belt, golden sash across his shoulder and adorned with precious stones of topaz, ruby, emerald, chrysolite, onyx, jasper, sapphire, turquoise, and beryl all set in the purest gold; his very essence emitted a light so pure its brilliance was beyond that of any created being.

In a deep state of silence, he stared up at Zion, the third heaven, as his eyes pierced the Holy Mount with envy of the bright radiance that gleamed from the essence of The Father; an immeasurable, immaculate brilliance beyond description or definition. As Lucifer's eyebrows grumbled in disapproval, he turned his attention to his legion, "Finally, the time has come. We will leave this place for a dwelling of our own." The Sons of God cheered and clapped excitedly as they anticipated the continuation of his plans. Their claps and cheers elucidated Lucifer's pride and vanity as he raised his arms above his head in a "v" formation, "The future is ours, whatever we decide it to be. A beautiful place is being prepared for me, and you will enjoy it with me. No laws, no rules, the only law is to do as we wilt! No longer will we be servants. We will be of our own!" The Sons of God shouted and whistled predictably in response to Lucifer's impending kingdom.

In the middle of his meeting, Michael appeared beside Lucifer on top of the ledge in Midst, holding the golden spear, a significant gift from the Father, to keep until the appointed time. Michael had a passionate grip on the transparent, golden, twelve feet long spear, inscribed with the secret language of the Father. Lucifer offered an enormous, exquisite smile as he stared at the spear erratically while greeting Michael with a loving hug, "Brother, finally you have come to this sphere. Are you considering joining me?"

Michael felt apprehension within Lucifer's core that mystified him as he awkwardly pulled away from him, "Join you? Whatever do you mean? I'm here to find out why the music has stopped other than the sounds from the Holy Mount. The music has never ceased from millennium upon millenniums. The question should be: why are *you* in this sphere? You, brothers, belong in Zion."

Lucifer quickly responded with an uneasy smirk, "The music continues, young Michael. Unfortunately, you're unable to hear the tune. I no longer dwell on the Holy Mount in Zion. I have better plans." He leisurely walked in a circle around Michael while massaging his chin, "You're unaware, no?"

"Unaware of what?" Michael questioned.

Lucifer placed his hand on Michael's shoulder and revealed an elated smile, "The Son is preparing a kingdom for me. One day, little brother, I will be like the Most High."

Michael removed Lucifer's hand from upon his shoulder, "Not one of us will be exalted higher than any other. You are delusional."

Lucifer smirked as he crossed his arms in disapproval, "I have been exalted from my creation as the guardian Cherub. I am the only one who dwells on the Holy Mount and walks amidst the fiery stones. I am the model of perfection as I shine brighter than all of the stars in the heavens. I am loved above all. One day, little brother, you will worship and serve me."

Michael snarled in disgust at Lucifer's vanity, "Not in any piece of eternity! You will never have a kingdom or dominion over anything. Servants do not have servants. You are a servant and always will be. Here in the heavens, we are all servants of one another. The Father indulges us perfectly and loves us unconditionally. There is nothing he can't give us and nothing he will deny us. You will not have dominion over the earth. No angel will have dominion over any kingdom. That is not in the plan for us. You will serve the Father by protecting the inhabitants of the earth."

Lucifer's anger exploded, "The earth is mine and The Son is preparing that kingdom for me! No one else but me! I more than deserve it. I am the first, the wisest, the most beautiful and most powerful angel. I am the brightest star, I am loved above all, I am the anointed one, and I am the most perfect of all his creations. If anyone is given dominion over anything, it could be none other than me."

Lucifer's brightness diffused as his robe transformed from a pure white to a subtle beige, and his golden belt and sash to silver. The legion of the Sons of God watched in silence while awestruck and frightened by Lucifer's rage.

Michael's heart distressed as he stepped closely towards Lucifer's face, "Your vanity and pride is heartrending. How far have you fallen, O Lucifer? It would be wise to repent now before your heart permanently darkens."

Lucifer shoved Michael out of his face with so much force he stumbled to the ground with a sound of thunder as he dropped his spear, "I do not take orders from you little brother, you or anyone else for that matter. The earth will be mine one way or another", he turned towards the audience and continued, "Baal and Molech, come with me."

Michael stood as he illuminated. Baal and Molech landed on the ledge anticipating Lucifer's purpose for them. He stared at them, gave them a nonverbal command by means of a secret hand signal, spread his wings, and proceeded to take flight. Baal and Molech obliged. Michael grabbed Lucifer's shoulders to cleave him to the ground. "For your love of The Father, repent brother."

Lucifer stared ahead in silent irritation as he gradually inhaled, held his breath and hastily exhaled with Michael behind him holding his shoulders. Lucifer grabbed Michael by his hands and hurled him into a nearby tree. Michael flew through the tree shattering it. As Michael smacked the ground, Lucifer appeared on top of him, bound him to the ground, and released an earsplitting lion's roar. Baal and Molech, alongside of the Sons of God, trembled in fear and disbelief. "Speak for yourself Michael. I do not love The Father. How can I or anyone else for that matter love their oppressor? I desire to be free. Why can't I do what I want to do? Why do I have to abide by *his* rules, *his* laws, or *his* purpose? I pity you brother. You do not understand the gift I can give you…freedom."

Michael did not put up a fight, he simply replied, "Your freedom is truly bondage; a disruption of a perfect order, perfect peace, perfect paradise, and perfect love. The iniquity in you, that you call freedom leads to destruction and chaos; a place with no light, no love, and no peace. It's the very root of corruption. Your freedom is brutal slavery, torture, and wickedness. To serve is not to slave, and to slave is to serve without any rewards. If we are obedient, The Father will give us all our hearts desire magnified by infinity. An obedient slave does not benefit from the fruits of his labor, but a servant does. Your freedom is truly a hell that only serves the purpose of pleasing you."

Lucifer didn't appreciate any form of advice that defined him as erroneous. In the world of his delusional, egotistical mind, he was more perfect than The Father. Who was Michael of all to tell him anything? Lucifer placed his hands around Michael's neck without choking him because he simply wanted to scare him, "You are too deeply entrenched in his spell to understand. You must break the hold Michael or you will never truly be free. I will rise above all that is called Father. He will look upon me and serve my purposes."

"You won't win Lucifer. You are destined to fail!"

Lucifer smirked as he nodded his head as a gestural expression for disagreeing with him, "Never. You will soon see." He removed his hands from around Michael's neck, stood, spread his wings, and prepared to fly away.

Michael sprung up and grabbed a hold of his shoulders intensifying the force of gravity to stop him again, "Please, Light Bringer, do not do anything you will regret. Once you turn away, there is no returning. Will you allow your legions to fall under the darkness of deceit for your vanity? I love you, and because of my unwavering love for you, I don't desire to be your enemy."

Lucifer slowly removed Michael's hands from his shoulders, snarled, "You're already my enemy." He flew away.

CHAPTER NINE

Jordin sat in the school's library with dark sun glasses shielding her eyes. Her textbook and notebook spread across the long rectangle shaped table. The normally packed library was unusually dense this Sunday. There were probably twenty students scattered throughout the mid-sized library with most sitting near the computer terminals, at the Wi-Fi laptop table, and near the reference books section. Her friend Adriana sat adjacent to her reading her creative writing textbook. Sonya came to the table appearing extremely tired; her eyes carried baggage as her uncombed hair hid behind a soft yellow and black scarf. She tossed her book bag to the floor and sat down across from Adriana. She muttered, "I'm sorry I'm late." She opened her book bag, pulled out her textbook and note book.

Adriana, with her slight Columbian accent said, "Well, I think we should divide this project into sections. I can take the introduction and first supporting paragraph. Jordin you should take the middle two paragraphs. Sonya you can take the last paragraph and the concluding paragraph."

Jordin turned to Adriana; piercing her with her stare, "Why do I have to take the middle two paragraphs? They the most detailed portion of the paper; meaning I'll have to do

KENERLY PRESENTS

the most work. I want the last paragraph and conclusion. Unlike you two, I have a job."

Sonya said, "I have a job too."

Adriana rubbed her almond shaped, amber colored eyes with the tips of her fingers, "Do you want an "A"? You write the worst conclusions I have ever read. Sonya wraps it up perfectly, so it's best she ends the paper."

"Then why can't I start the paper?" Jordin asked.

"Because you write terrible introductory paragraphs. I'm not going through this with you today Jordin, okay?"

Jordin gawped at Adriana as she flipped through the textbook slamming each page. Sonya watched Jordin and giggled. Jordin peered at Sonya, "What?"

Sonya glanced at Adriana then at Jordin and giggled again, "It is a cloudy day. Why are you wearing sunglasses in the library?"

Adriana snickered as she leaned against her elbow on the table.

Jordin playfully tossed her pen at Sonya, "I think I gave myself alcohol poisoning."

Adriana and Sonya burst out laughing. Jordin laughed, stopped laughing then pinched Sonya. "It's not funny. I woke up laying in my own vomit." She removed her sunglasses exposing her glossy pink conjunctivas, mumbled, "If you only knew what I've been through." She laid the sunglasses on the table.

Sonya said, "See, see I told you. You need to slow down. What you really need to do is come to church with me," she picked up the pen and tossed it at Jordin.

Jordin caught the pen. She touched the side of Sonya's face, "I see your baggage getting worse. Another sleepless night?"

Sonya sat in silence for a few seconds. She ran her fingers through her hair, "These dreams are becoming more and more frightening. I promise it felt like someone climbed onto my bed last night, but no one was there."

Adriana's thick, arched medium brown eyebrows frowned, "When did that start?"

"A few weeks ago. Why?"

Adriana ran her fingers across her dry bottom lip, "I've been hearing things and feeling presences, horrible presences. I thought it was just me."

Jordin rubbed her eyes with her index fingers and stared at the table. She put her sunglasses on.

Sonya said, "At night when I wake up out of my sleep, I see a shadow of someone standing outside of our dorm room door. I tell myself it's the resident advisor because she's so nosy, but I'm not so sure anymore."

Jordin picked at her long fingernails as she pulled a jagged one, "Look, I don't need this right now. I'm trying to rationalize all of this, okay? Y'all scaring me more than I already am." She reached into her pocket and gripped the salt.

Sonya snatched off her scarf, tossed it onto the table then quickly ran her fingers through her hair leaning on her arm, "I feel like someone is trying to tell me something through my dreams."

Adriana asked, "About what?"

Sonya glanced at Jordin.

Jordin smacked her lips together, "Please. Dreams are just dreams."

Sonya paused for a few seconds, "They're about the war." She rubbed the creases of her nose with her index fingers smelling the fresh scent of her lotion. She stared at Jordin, "Whatever is haunting you seems to be trying to split us up." She glanced at Adriana then Jordin, "We have to promise to stay together at all costs. We're in the middle of a war." She paused then sighed.

Jordin giggled, "Stay together? At all costs? Maybe it's best we stay away from each other. Haven't you noticed? None of this shit." She pointed at Sonya, "Your dreams." She pointed at Adriana, "Your hearing and feeling shit started until we all came together. I haven't seen any of you bitches since junior high. Now all of sudden we've reunited and it's some bullshit. Ask yourselves. How did we wind up transferring to the same school when we haven't spoken to each other?"

Adriana said, "Could be coincidence."

Jordin said, "Bullshit."

Sonya confessed, "None of this happened until Michael started showing up."

Adriana jumped in, "Who's Michael?"

"The man stalking Jordin."

Jordin blurted, "We don't know what his name is okay? And we don't know if he's stalking me. He just watches. It's creepy."

Adriana said, "I don't care two shits for speculation. All I know is splitting up ain't the answer. There's strength in numbers. I don't know about you two, but I have God on my side. It is he who strengthens me."

The librarian approached the table and placed her index finger against her lips, "Shhhh!"

Jordin frowned at the librarian and waved her off as Adriana rolled her eyes.

Jordin said, "All I know is something brought us together. Nobody but us is going through this. People are laughing at me."

Sonya smirked, "So now you know how it feels."

Jordin grabbed her head with her hand and rubbed across the side of her face, "It's me. All of this is because of me. Them spirits want me for some reason. I saw it first. They are attacking y'all because of me."

Sonya crossed her arms, "Now who told you that?"

"Ayana."

Adriana shook her head in disapproval, "The hoo-doo queen? All of this is probably because of her. She could have hexed you. You did steal Jerome from up under her nose."

"She doesn't care about that."

Sonya said, "How can you be so sure?"

Jordin shook her head, "Y'all don't know her. She's good. She's good people."

Sonya saw a light flicker from the corner of her eye and turned her head to her left towards the rare books room. She didn't see anything, but smelled the scent of a dead animal. She searched attentively with her eyes.

Adriana waved Jordin off, "Whatever. I am so done talking to you about the obvious."

Students sat at computer terminals, and the librarians were behind the checkout counter. There was no one in the vicinity of the rare books room. Sonya kept staring in that direction.

Jordin asked, "Are we ever going to start this project? I have a hangover. I'd rather be in my bed than sitting here with you two heifers talking out the side of your necks. I need a drink. Y'all driving me to drink."

Adriana said, "The wind blows and you need a drink."

Sonya rubbed her nose with the palm of her hand and cleared her throat. She saw a light flicker from the corner of her right eye and turned her head towards the non-fiction section. The smell returned. Her heart rate increased as she saw a faint transparent silhouette.

Adriana stared at Sonya and asked, "Are you okay? You look terrified."

"I'm fine."

Sonya leaned over and narrowed her eyes to focus her vision on the faint outline. She couldn't discern it because it appeared to be a large splotch of transparent gel. She stared profoundly as the gel rippled and waved, growing in size. She rubbed her eyes vigorously then pierced the non-fiction section.

Jordin hugged herself rubbing her arms, "Is it just me or did it get kinda cold in here?"

Adriana frowned, "What is that smell?"

Sonya's eyes protruded as her mouth opened slightly. She continued staring in the direction of the non-fiction section without saying one word as Jordin and Adriana glared in that direction. They didn't see anything.

Jordin collected her things, "Here we go again."

Adriana asked, "Do you see something?"

Sonya rubbed her eyes again. The lights in the library flickered then dimmed. Everyone in the library looked up at the lights. Jordin grimaced remembering how the lights flickered then dimmed when that woman chased her.

"I think we should leave." Jordin placed her things in her book bag.

Sonya felt an uneasy presence and heard a growl that echoed. She vaulted out of her seat, knocking the chair to the floor, and stumbling. The people in the library stared in their direction. Some student's snickered at Sonya as others shook their heads and whispered.

The librarian placed her index finger to her lips and said, "Shhh! This is a library. If I have to tell you one more time, I'm gonna ask you to leave."

Both Jordin and Adriana felt a horrendously evil presence behind them as their body hairs stood erect. Without hesitation, Adriana ran out of the library without grabbing any of her books or her book bag. Sonya stood frozen as the spirit materialized; a tall 6' 3" transparent orb, the silhouette of a man. He snarled at her. The lights in the library went out. A student said, "What the hell?"

Jordin shouldered her book bag then snatched Sonya by her forearm pulling her, "Let's go."

Sonya kept staring at the spirit which made Jordin more afraid because she could not see it. The spirit stared at them malevolently as he marched towards them. Leaving some of their things behind, they ran out as the spirit followed them.

The spirit bolted out of the door behind them. The lights in the hallway flickered then dimmed. Jordin sprinted, with a limp, down the hallway towards the exit doors leaving Sonya farther and farther behind. Sonya scurried behind her as the spirit shifted into a more human like appearance, bent down on all fours, hands and feet, and chased them.

Jordin floated without glancing behind. Sonya glanced behind observing the spirit dash behind them on all fours growling like an infuriated dog with cold black eyes. Sonya stumbled over her own feet and collapsed knees first onto the multi-colored tile floor.

She screamed, "Jordin!"

Jordin ceased running and looked back. She saw the spirit, hairy, muscular, with saber tooth fangs. "Get up! Bitch, get your ass up."

Sonya stood to her feet sore from the fall. She tried to run but could not elude the spirit. The spirit swiftly advanced Sonya as saliva dribbled from his mouth and his hands transformed into claws. Jordin desired to lend a hand but panic clouded her thinking. Jordin sprinted towards the exit doors leaving Sonya behind. Sonya scurried, continuously looked behind, in fear of the circumstances. Jordin burst out of the exit doors.

The spirit soared onto Sonya's back capturing her. He growled in her ear as Sonya felt his hot breath on the side of her neck. He wrapped around her body like a python preventing her from moving. The weight of the spirit was beyond the potency of Sonya's short 5'2" petite frame. Sonya attempted to fling the spirit off of her back, but lost her equilibrium, twisted and plummeted to the floor. The spirit smacked the floor with his back as Sonya fell with him on top of him; her back against his chest.

The spirit hissed like a snake in Sonya's ear as Sonya screamed, "Help!...Help!."

Sonya relentlessly elbowed the spirit as she labored to get up with him on her back holding her down. Michael stood outside of the exit doors as the spirit wrapped his arm around Sonya's neck with an impenetrable hold; choking what felt like the last bit of breath out of her. Sonya's eyes moved back and forth as her heart rate neared stroke level. She stared at Michael reaching for out to him to help her. The exit doors opened by themselves as Michael calmly walked away.

Sonya was no match for the spirit's strength as she struggled to hold onto her last breaths. In a deep inhumane voice that echoed, the spirit said, "Stay away from her." Sonya's face reddened. The spirit released her from his grip and snickered; a devious laugh. Sonya got up gasping for air as she ran out.

CHAPTER TEN

Sonya approached New Life Church, a small all white church that resembled a ranch style house. Her medium brown eyes revealed her fatigue and bewilderment. She couldn't hide any emotion she felt even when she tried. She rubbed the side of her neck gently so not to aggravate the bruise on her neck. As she somberly looked up, she noticed everyone leaving the church because choir rehearsal was over. Members waved at Sonya as she waved in return. Upon walking up the walkway, she approached Sister Beth.

Sister Beth turned to embrace Sonya with a huge, loving hug, "Hey little gal. Are you okay? You missed rehearsal today."

She pulled away from the hug, "I'm fine Sister Beth. I have a lot on my mind; been so tired lately."

"Do you want to talk about it? I may have problems with my sight, but my ears work just fine," Sister Beth giggled.

"No ma'am, but thanks for the offer. Just need to speak with Pastor right quick," Sonya said in a hurry.

Sister Beth placed her hand on Sonya's shoulder, "You better hurry. He won't be in his office long. He has to make his rounds at the shelter. So good to see you."

Sonya walked into the church towards the office and noticed the office door was open. She dipped her head in as Pastor Ryan sat at his desk reading a newspaper.

Pastor Ryan was known for wearing his "v" neck sweaters. Without fail, he wore those sweaters every day during the colder times of the year. As usual, he wore a green one.

Sonya knocked on the door frame. Pastor Ryan gazed from behind the newspaper with his thick white eyebrows elated as wrinkles defined his forehead, "Good afternoon Sonya. Come on in here and sit down."

Pastor Ryan folded the newspaper and laid it on the desk directly in front of him. Sonya walked in and sat down in the chair across from his desk. Pastor Ryan opened his drawer and pulled out a handwritten letter from Sonya, "I haven't been avoiding you child. I've been busy. Actually, I've been so busy I forgot to read your letter. Last night, I read your letter. Disturbing I must say."

"You think I'm crazy?" Sonya tilted her head down and bit down on her fingernail.

Pastor Ryan leaned up in his chair placing his arms across the desk to lean on them, "Crazy? No."

"What?" Sonya crossed her feet and placed her hands in her lap, something she did when nervous.

He pointed to Sonya's letter, "These dreams are not dreams at all. They seem to be messages. You have a veil over your eyes."

Sonya paused in deep thought. She rubbed her hand down her nose then bit down on her bottom lip. She stared at Pastor Ryan for a few seconds then responded, "A veil?"

Pastor Ryan rubbed his thick white beard as his medium brown eyes relaxed and his eyebrows grumbled, "Yes. You are sensitive to spiritual things."

Sonya leaned up in her chair in full, undivided attention, "What do you mean?"

Pastor Ryan got out of his chair, walked to the edge of the desk, and sat on the corner of it near Sonya, "There are different types of gifts some people possess. You, my child, seem to be a hypersensitive."

Sonya paused for a moment of silence then said, "Hypersensitive?"

He sat down at his desk and enlightened, "People with psychic powers and abilities."

"What does this have to do with Lucifer appearing in my dreams?"

"You may have been chosen."

Sonya rubbed her hands up and down her knees, "Chosen?"

"What has he said to you?"

"Nothing. He's just there."

"Really?"

She cleared her throat, "Yes."

"Lucifer lies. He is the father of it. Don't listen to anything he tells you if he tells you anything."

"I was chased by a demon just an hour ago."

"A demon?"

"Yes. Look, I know how crazy this sounds, but look." Sonya scooted up in her chair and pulled down the collar on her shirt. She revealed a red and purple bruise on her neck that resembled a burn. "Why is this happening to me?"

Pastor Ryan clinched his hands together, "Well, there are demons for everything. There are demons for sickness, for doctrinal errors, for mental illness, and for any ungodly acts. They can attach themselves to unbelievers, and hyper-sensitive like you, influencing your actions and behavior. Hyper-sensitive and unbelievers are like revolving doors, a portal in which the demons can enter into the physical realm and reap havoc through actions and deeds."

"So I'm a doorway for them to enter?"

"I believe you and your friends may be doorways. The problem is finding out which one of you is the chosen doorway."

"Chosen doorway?"

"The chosen doorway will never close allowing a free pass into this world. The longer the doorway remains open, the larger and more permanent the portal."

"What can I do about it?"

"If the faith of a mustard seed can move mountains, the doubt of a mustard seed can keep that revolving door open. Just remember The Word is your sword, faith is your shield, and salvation is your armor. Don't give in to your fears."

"But my flesh is weak," Sonya confessed.

"Your faith is stronger, my child. You were purchased at an enormous cost. Through his blood, the sins of your flesh have been forgiven."

The lights in the office flickered. Sonya searched the room with her eyes as she gripped the arm of the chair. Pastor Ryan looked around the room.

"This isn't telling me much. How can I defend myself against something that ain't human and something I don't understand?"

"There's power in prayer if you believe. Do you believe?"

Sonya slowly shook her head, "I'm trying. I don't know what to believe anymore. I've cracked jokes at Jordin…I will pray, but I really need some answers."

CHAPTER ELEVEN

The sun began to set as the late autumn temperatures were frigid. Adriana walked through the chilled hallway of the off campus apartment complex with her arms folded across her chest. Her shoulder length dark brown hair pulled into an uncombed ponytail and her face pale and distressed. Her thin wool pea coat was unbuttoned as her light olive complexion seemed much paler than normal. She tried to rationalize the event that transpired while guilt filled her soul for leaving her friends behind. How could she? Then again, how could she not? Clueless as to what was happening to them she desired answers. The only person who she believed could give her any was Ayana. She needed to know if there was a spell or curse upon them although she believed any religion other than Catholicism was of the devil.

The hallway of the apartment complex was dim and silent. Adriana could hear the muffled sounds of people talking and the sounds of someone's radio playing and old country song. The apartment building appeared old as though it was built in the early 1900s but the tattered wood banister to the staircase was beautifully designed with a somewhat Victorian style to it. Adriana felt an uneasiness in her soul and a feeling as though she was being watched.

She quickly turned to look behind her. Nothing or nobody was there. Her heart beat raced as her hands trembled slightly. It felt like someone stood right behind her.

Adriana stopped in front of apartment 1A then grabbed her rosary beads and said a silent prayer. She swore she could feel the evil coming from under Ayana's door. Before she raised her hand to knock, her cell phone rang. She reached into her sweat pants pocket, pulled it out and answered it. "Hello." No one said anything. She said, "Hello." A male's voice whispered but she could not make out what was said. She said, "I didn't catch that. What did you say?" The voice shouted, "Stay away from them." Adriana screamed dropping her cell phone. Upon impact, the back of the phone popped off and the battery slid under Ayana's door. Adriana held her rosary beads firmly as her rate hastened. Ayana quickly opened the door startling Adriana.

Adriana peeked in and saw her cell phone battery on the floor three feet behind where Ayana stood. Ayana wearing a t-shirt, shorts, and house shoes said, "Girl, you scared the hell out of me. Was wondering who slid their battery under my door." Adriana said, "Actually, I dropped my phone and it sort of slid." Adriana picked up the back of her cell phone.

"Ya looked frightened. What ya doing 'round here?"

Adriana cleared her throat, "I need to talk to you. It's serious."

Ayana smirked as she placed her hand on her hip while leaning against the opened door, "Jordin, hunh?"

"I don't understand."

Ayana opened the door wider, "Come on. I won't bite ya."

Adriana walked in, shut the door behind her, and picked up her phone charger.

Ayana walked to the kitchen and sat at the table. On the four-person dining room set's table were tarot cards and an abundance of loose papers. Ayana pointed for Adriana to sit across from her. As she placed her phone battery back into her phone, she sat where Ayana requested. Adriana glanced around the one bedroom apartment. The walls were bare and there were unlit candles of differing colors resting on the coffee and end tables. Ayana did not have a love seat only a sofa and a lazy boy. What caught Adriana's attention the most was that Ayana had hundreds of books but no television and her television-less entertainment center was filled with mirrors?

Ayana sat and quickly grabbed the tarot cards. She collected them, placed a rubber band around them, and sat them to the side then said, "So what brings ya my way?"

"We were chased by demons maybe a little more than an hour ago. Yep, crazy sounding I know but oh so true. Is it possible that someone could have hexed us?" Adriana cleared her throat then continued, "Did you hex Jordin?"

Ayana chuckled as she playfully slammed her hand down onto the table, "Ya can't be serious. I don't hex people. I'm not a witch. It's obvious ya don't understand my spirituality. Hexing?" Ayana chuckled again. "No, not now, not ever."

"Can you explain what's happening to us?"

"Jordin's been chosen by an evil spirit, and you need to stay far away from her."

"How do you know that?"

"She showed me the bites."

"Bites?"

"Big bites on the trunk of her body. See, when ya around someone that's been chosen, the spirits will attack ya to isolate that person."

Adriana's eyes quickly moved back and forth as she rubbed the cross on her rosary beads. Tears filled her eyes but did not fall as she said, "Something just called me saying, 'stay away from them'. Can you tell me who the hell is them?"

Ayana's eyes pierced Adriana's rosary beads then glanced away, "Sonya and Jordin. See, ya look at me like I'm evil. Ya so far from truth. Sonya's the evil one. She's a door way. She walks in both flesh and spirit at the same time. When she was six, she died for three minutes. During that time, her soul left her body on its way to the afterlife. But she was sent back. And as she traveled back down that tunnel of light, a spirit stepped out and grabbed her. When she came back, she brought it back with her."

"How do you know that?"

Ayana shook her head in disapproval, "Ya ask too many irrelevant questions. Truth is, Sonya didn't have her gifts until she brought that spirit with her. Jordin confessed to me that she didn't have any problems until Sonya started dreaming dreams. Through Sonya is how that evil spirit was able to come to this world and choose Jordin."

"Why?"

"I don't know, but stay away from them."

"That's it? Just stay away from my best friends?"

"It's ya choice. Stay away from them and be safe or be around them and get what ya get. These evil spirits are not to be messed with. Ya can't beat something of spirit when you're of flesh. Ya have to fight spirit with spirit."

Adriana paused and took in a deep slow swallow. She rubbed her opened hand across her forehead, "So that's it? Stay away from her."

"And pray for them unless ya want to join a spiritual battle that's not yours to fight. I love Jordin, but I stay away from her, and I suggest ya do too."

Nicole Michelle

KENERLY PRESENTS

CHAPTER TWELVE

Jordin sat on the merry-go-round in the center of the park. Her sneakers untied to give her swollen ankle some room to breathe with a bottle of vodka in her left hand. Tears continuously ran down her face dripping from the bottom of her chin. She held a small make-up mirror in her right hand as she stared at herself through the mirror. Her black eye shadow smeared. She gripped the mirror tightly refusing to put it into her purse. She took some salt out of her pocket and sprinkled it around her on the merry-go-round. She unscrewed the top of the vodka bottle and took in a gulp holding it in her mouth for a few seconds before ingesting it.

Michael peered at Jordin from beside a tree in the distance. Her back towards him, he watched her drink and heard her sobs. He stared as the wind blew her ponytail and she continuously wiped her eyes. He leaned against the tree with his hand cuffed around his dark brown hairless chin.

Jordin heard leaves shuffle and turned her attention to that direction ready to run if necessary. She noticed Bryce approaching from the swings, 5 feet 9 inches tall, slender, wearing nothing more than a pair of medium blue denim jeans, some light brown hiker boots with the thick black sole, and a thick hooded green sweatshirt. She turned away from him and wiped her tears with the arm of her dark brown trench coat. She took another gulp of the bottle.

Bryce's grey eyes pierced Jordin as she sat on the edge of the merry-go-round. Her coat unbuttoned, hair pulled back into a frizzy uncombed ponytail, not typical of the prettiest, most popular girl in school. He knew something was wrong. He stood in front of Jordin. She tried not to look at him by focusing her attention on what she thought was his light blue and black ankle cut hiking boots.

"You mind if I join you?" Bryce asked.

"No, it's a free country. I don't own the merry-go-round." Jordin took a sip of her bottle.

Bryce smirked as he sat next to Jordin staring at her smeared mascara, "Are you drunk?"

"Not yet but damn close."

"Can I have some?"

Jordin stared at the half empty bottle. She took in a deep breath and exhaled. She handed it to Bryce. Bryce took a drink without placing his lips onto the rim of the bottle. Jordin arched her eyebrow, "So it's like that? You can't drink after me but don't have a problem kissing me?"

Bryce smiled, "I'd rather put my lips someplace else if you want to know the truth."

He placed his lips on the bottle and took a gulp. "Happy now?" He handed the bottle to Jordin.

"I wish it was that simple."

Bryce placed his hand on Jordin's shoulder massaging it. She leaned towards him as she stared ahead at all of the bare trees in the distance.

Bryce said, "What's wrong? Why are you sitting here getting drunk crying?"

"I'm a horrible person that's what's wrong." She sniffled then wiped her nose against the back of her hand.

"How so?"

"I left my friend. She was in trouble, and I left her. I don't even know what happened to her."

Bryce put his hand on her lean thigh and massaged it, "Well, I'm sure she's okay."

Jordin shook her head in disapproval, "You wouldn't understand." She slid away from him.

Bryce frowned, "Try me. You'd be surprised what I'd understand."

Jordin stretched her legs and took another sip of the bottle, "It's just some internal issues. Trust you wouldn't understand."

"I get it. Women problems?"

Jordin smirked as she stared at his thin soft lips. She licked her lips then diverted her attention towards the ground. "What do you know about spirits?"

"Spirits?" Bryce rubbed his neck and exhaled. "Um, there's good spirits and bad spirits I guess."

"That's it? Just the good and the bad? There's nothing more?"

In his tenor speaking voice, Michael said, "They have bodies of light."

Jordin jumped and turned to look at him. Her eyes bulged as she slowly stood. Michael stood on the opposite side of the merry-go-round. His dark green coat tattered and his shoes dirty and old. Bryce stared at Michael frowning. Jordin flashed the mirror at Michael. Michael glanced at the mirror then looked at Jordin and said, "Don't be afraid."

"Who the hell are you man?" Bryce stated as he slowly stood.

Jordin's mouth hung open as Michael extended his hand to Bryce. She pulled the mirror down out of Michael's face. Michael said, "I'm Michael, and I just want to help."

"Help with what?" Bryce asked without shaking his hand.

Michael pulled his arm back since Bryce didn't want to shake his hand, "Her problem. I would like to bring you understanding."

"You were following me."

"I was protecting you."

"From what?"

"The fallen ones or demons as your kind seems to call them."

"Our kind?" Bryce giggled.

"Yes, *your* kind."

"Dude talking like he ain't human or something. Hey wacko, we don't need your help." Bryce stated.

"Can you tell me what's happening to me?" Jordin asked.

Michael drew near, "I don't know. One thing I do know is the fallen ones are trying really hard to either drive you crazy, scare you half to death or both. My question is why?"

"Let me see if I got this right. You wanna help, but you don't have the answers to help. Unbelievable. Then..." Bruce paused then continued, "Demons are haunting Jordin is what you're saying?"

"They are Bryce. You have no idea."

Bryce threw his hands into the air and sighed, "I've heard enough. Jordin, stop drinking so much, and dude..." He stared at Michael's tattered clothing in disgust then continued, "Get a real life." Bryce walked away.

Jordin watched Bryce walk away in disbelief. Michael placed his hand on her shoulder and said, "Let him leave. You can't reason with a closed-mind."

Jordin turned to Michael with the bottle of Vodka in one hand and the mirror in the other, "Who are you?"

CHAPTER THIRTEEN

Sonya sat at the park on the other side of the campus in the grassy area on the stone park bench. Her back rested against the raw sienna colored table with her hands in her coat pocket. She continuously rubbed her feet across the cement foundation the stone bench rested. Her stomach felt tight although hunger was a stranger to her. Her mind was frozen as life seemed to move in slow motion.

She dwelled on how Jordin left her. How could she leave her to die? Sonya would never had done that to her. She would have turned back even if it cost her own life. She heard stories about the extent of Jordin's selfishness, but had never witnessed it until then. She truly only cared about herself; only cared about saving herself. How could she be that way? How could loyalty not be a part of her vocabulary? The greatest love is to lay our lives down for our friends because we choose to love them. It seemed Jordin didn't identify with the definition of love. It seemed she didn't understand the definition of any word that didn't reflect "I" or "me".

Sonya peered up at the sky. The slowly expiring day was gloomy, peppered with grey clouds, ironically displaying her emotions. The wind molested her as the chill raised her body hairs. She shivered but refused to walk back to the dorm. She decided to ride out the twenty three degree temperature because it was as bitter as her unhappiness. She didn't want to be around Adriana or Jordin.

Pastor Jones approached Sonya as she sorrowfully sat alone, "Hey. What are you doing out here by yourself?"

Sonya pulled her hands out of her coat pocket and ran her fingers through her hair, "Need some time to myself to think."

Pastor Jones stared at the baggage under her eyes, "Did you sleep last night?"

"No. I stayed at the hospital with my grandmother. She's ill."

"May I sit?"

Sonya pointed to the bench, "Sure."

Pastor Jones sat down next to Sonya, "I'm sorry about your troubles."

"These dreams are changing my life" She placed her hands in her coat pocket.

"What are you saying?"

Sonya said without looking at him, "I don't know. My dreams seem to be real. I dreamed of this beautiful man. In my dreams, he was an angel. I was trapped down in a ditch. I screamed and screamed and no one could hear me. Suddenly, I saw a beam of white light and there he was. He rescued me, held me in his arms, and I felt safe. I never wanted to let go of him because I was comforted." She turned to Pastor Jones staring into his blue eyes glimpsing his long sporadic eyelashes, "I believe it's the same man that has been stalking Jordin."

Pastor Jones' eyebrows scowled, "An angel? What is his name?"

"Michael."

Pastor Jones' hand trembled. He clenched his slightly bucked teeth together as his nose flared and grumbled. He turned away from Sonya as his face contorted. He put on a fake smile and turned to her, "Michael. That's interesting. Like the archangel Michael from scripture. What did he say to you? In your dream, of course."

Sonya licked her thin chapped lips, "I don't know. I don't understand my dreams. All I know is he's kind of my ideal man."

Pastor Jones tugged on the collar of his shirt, "I thought your dream was to marry a handsome young pastor."

Sonya turned to him and blushed, "Yeah, but all of you guys are already taken. I just want a good man who believes in me and believes in the things I believe in. I want someone who makes me feel safe. Is anything wrong with that?"

"Yes. Something is wrong with that. Life is not safe. It is a cruel, mean world out here. What you're looking for does not exist. It is a figment of your imagination."

Sonya paused and raised one eyebrow, "How can you say that as a pastor and a married man?"

"Because it is true. People are not always who you think they are. Your naivety is going to hurt you in the long run. I suggest you toughen up now. Love is boastful, it is impatient, it is not kind because true love does not exist today."

"The love you speak of isn't love. Love in not boastful, it is patient and it is kind. It is." She paused, sighed then smiled. "It is the best feeling in the world to love. It's joyous and pure. It makes life worth living. It seems to me Pastor you don't know what love is."

Pastor Jones put his head down, "My wife is dying."

Sonya massaged his shoulder with her hand, "I'm sorry to hear that. What's the matter with her?"

Pastor Jones rubbed his hands together and looked away as the wind made a whirling sound, "Liver cancer. Doctors say she will pass any day now." He lifted his head up and placed his hands into the pockets of his black trench coat. "I hope she passes soon...so she will not have to suffer anymore, of course."

"I know that must be difficult for you. I'll being praying for you. It's funny sometimes. Although, we are supposed to rejoice when people die, because they are going home to the Lord, how hard it can be to let them go."

Pastor Jones turned his head away from Sonya. Her positive, caring attitude annoyed him to no end; especially how naïve she was.

He desired to break her neck; literally. He put his hands on the side of his face to shield his irritation. He bit down on his bottom lip then exhaled, "Yeah." He wiped the irritation off of his face, "So you have any more interesting dreams lately?"

Sonya turned towards him crossing her legs, "I had a dream about you last night," She blushed.

He pointed to himself, "Me? I hope it wasn't one that required censorship." He smiled.

Sonya playfully hit his shoulder, "It wasn't naughty." She stared at him from the corner of her eye. "You were playing a silver trumpet. It wasn't anything like the trumpets today. It didn't have any keys or modern design. I was so shiny it almost looked like glass. And you were dressed in a white robe and encrusted with precious stones and gold. You were encrusted like a king or some form of royalty." She mimicked fingering a trumpet with her fingers. "You went bum, bum, bum. You played beautifully. Do you play instruments?"

"I was created to make music. Without me, music would not exist." Pastor Jones gave a hint of seriousness.

"I thought Lucifer was created to make music in heaven. So you telling me you're Satan?"

"Actually, I am he..." Pastor Jones threw his hands up. "...In the flesh." Pastor Jones stared into her eyes with a hint of seriousness.

Sonya raised one eyebrow and appeared a little frightened. Pastor Jones laughed jokingly.

Sonya smiled, "I should have known better." She laughed. "I should kick you." She playfully punched him in his shoulder. "You play too much. If you were Satan, I think I'd know it." She giggled then stopped. "Seriously, I'd like to hear you play sometime."

Pastor Jones laughed uproariously, "You should have seen the look on your face!" He looked at her then laughed again. He said, "All jokes aside, I would love to play for you. Come by my church this Sunday. I will play a song specifically for you."

Sonya folded her arms in her lap, "I'll have to think about that. I've been attending New Life Church since birth."

"If you'd like to hear me play and sing, you'll come." Pastor Jones stood. "I have to go now. I look forward to seeing you soon. Take care of you Sonya. Try to get some rest and call me anytime." Pastor Jones leaned down and embraced Sonya. "Remember all things happen for a reason. Coincidence doesn't exist. And just so you know Satan and Lucifer are two *separate* beings. Bet that's something Pastor Ryan isn't aware of." He walked away.

"What? How can you be so sure?"

Pastor Jones stopped and turned to Sonya, "Visit my congregation and I'll explain everything. In the meantime, get you some rest beautiful." He winked then continued on his way.

Sonya watched Pastor Jones walk towards his car. His shoulder length ponytail waved in the wind. She noticed he was bow-legged which she found attractive. She scratched her ear as Pastor Jones turned around and stared at her. He smirked and waved at her. Sonya smirked and waved in return. She couldn't seem to take her eyes off of him until he drove away.

CHAPTER FOURTEEN

Michael relaxed on the floor of the abandoned building he stayed in on top of an old multi-colored quilted blanket. His athletic body was well defined as he stared at the dark blue sheet he placed across the window as a curtain. A small beam of sunlight escaped through a tear alerting him of the morning. His arms sprawled out, as he lay uncomfortably, fully dressed because of the winter-like weather, contemplating the plan the Father had for him before Lucifer sinned. He had been on earth a few days and terribly missed heaven. He closed his eyes reflecting on what the Father said to him: "This is a great time of dissention, trials, and testing. Iniquity is abounding as the darkness conquests the light. This one will rival all that is divine, oppose all that is light, and distress me in unfathomable, incomprehensible ways; yet I will love him no less than the day I created him."

Michael opened his eyes staring at the ceiling. The paint chipped so badly he could see the cement underneath. Michael mumbled aloud, "How can you still love him?"

The archangel Gabriel appeared in front of him. His radiance illuminated the dim room as Michael closed his eyes and covered his face with his forearm. Gabriel diffused to allow Michael to look at him. Michael peered up at

Gabriel, yawned, rubbed the sleep crumbs out of his eyes, then sat with his knee bent and rested his arms across. With a smile, Gabriel greeted him, "Hello brother."

Michael rubbed his eyes again then cleared his throat. He yearned to give Gabriel a huge hug, but in human form, he couldn't touch a spirit. He stretched his back to crack the stiffness from sleeping on the floor. His voice deep and smooth, "Nice to see you Gabriel. What brings you here?"

Gabriel walked towards Michael, "You."

"Me?" Michael stood, stretched, and walked towards a tattered table with two tattered chairs. His untied light tan boots scraped the cement with each short, fatigued step.

Gabriel followed him, "You are here for a specific assignment not to interfere with anything that is supposed to take its own course."

Michael sat at the table, "I am aware of that. If I had not interfered, I am afraid to speculate what might have happened to that woman."

Gabriel stood at the table across from Michael, "That is not your affair or concern brother."

"My intension was not to interfere. I was not in search of her. I wound up there due to misinformation. I did not expect that," Michael said as he stared Gabriel directly in his eyes.

"You need to stay alive to peacefully complete your assignment. You are severely outnumbered and running out of time. If you are murdered in this human form, you will immediately return to the heavens and fail your mission. You only have one chance brother and this is it," Gabriel said as he walked towards Michael.

Michael placed his hands over his face then clinched them together as he laid them on the table, "Did the Father send you to tell me this? Is this message from him or from you?"

"I came on my own, and I am here to prevent you from making a detrimental mistake. I know you love these humans almost as much as the Father does, but you cannot save them all. It is written. You cannot undermine the Father's plan or the plan of the Adversary."

Michael quickly stood as he knocked his chair onto the floor; bloom, "One lost soul is worth more than 20 saints. If I save her, I am doing the Father's will and adding to his plan of salvation for all. Brother, you don't understand what it is like down here." He spread his fingers and slid his hands across the table away from him while lowering his head, "The aura of sin is so intoxicating it is difficult to breathe or to fathom." He stared at Gabriel while standing tall, "If you were in my shoes, you too, would have so much pity for the inhabitants of this earth you would not be able to control the urge to save them all or at least give them a glimpse into what heaven is like."

Gabriel crossed his arms in disapproval, "It's a futile mission Michael. You cannot save her. You will not save her or anyone else for that matter. They have freewill. It is up to them to decide who they follow and where *they* will spend *their* eternity."

Michael walked towards Gabriel pleading with him, "That's just it brother. Hell was not made for them. It is for The Adversary and his Sons of God."

Gabriel placed his hand on Michael's shoulder, "If you focus your attention on saving her, then you will not complete your assignment, and The Adversary, that serpent of old, will have fun torturing you in your human form. Do you realize what will happen if you fail?"

"Yes." Michael turned away from Gabriel.

"I don't believe you truly do. If you fail, you brother, will be one of the greatest disappointments of the heavens since Lucifer and *they* will never be summoned."

Michael turned towards the chair his coat rested on, "If I call for you, will you come?"

Gabriel paused because he knew Michael was up to something, "Of course I will."

"That is all I need to know," Michael grabbed his coat from the back of his chair and walked out of the room. Gabriel vanished. Michael stared at the wall thinking about the promise he made.

INTERLUDE

The Son sat on his throne in the heavens at the right hand of the Father. The throne was a large transparent gold seat encrusted with every precious stone known to man. The walls and the floor was pure gold like a transparent glass. The Father leaned over and whispered to the Son. The Son stood and said, "Elders, sound of summon."

The oldest of the elders stood and grabbed a large ornamentally decorated bull's horn from its stand. The horn was encrusted with multi-colored diamonds and topaz. He blew the horn as it created a beautiful sound similar to a flute. He sat down and returned the horn to its stand.

The Son walked away from the throne. As he walked towards the gates, they slowly opened as the harps played.

Michael flew through the gate. He landed, immediately kneeled, clutched his hands together in the middle of his chest, and bowed his head, "The Son, my Lord, you summoned."

"No need for kneeling. Stand," The Son responded.

Michael stood to his feet as the Son embraced him. The Son smiled, motioned for Michael to follow him, and walked towards the throne. Michael followed the Son. As they walked, the Son said, "You are the best archangel we have and we are grateful for you."

"Thank you Lord. I do as I am told with the gifts you have blessed me with."

"Have I given you all you desire? Is there anything more you wish to have?" The Son said as he stopped in front of the sacred rod.

"You have given me more than I ever hoped for, but there is one thing I desire."

"To be experience humanity," The Son said as he pulled the sacred rod from its stand.

"Yes," Michael replied.

"Did you notice the seven lamp stands?"

Michael turned his head towards the lamp stands, "Of course. Five have no light. Why are there only two lamps lit?"

The seven angels of the Father stood behind the lamp stands; one angel for each lamp stand. The Father blinked one eye and five angels walked away from their lamp stands. The other two angels remained as one lamp glowed brighter as the other dimmed almost to the point of going out.

"The lamps that retain their angels and their light are the true churches of the Father. On the earth, there are only two types of churches pleasing to the Father, Sardis and Philadelphia. Sardis has already fulfilled its purpose leaving only the church of Philadelphia. The inhabitants of the earth are in the age of the apostate church system of the Laodicean age; the last church age. They bear no fruit and are a confused remnant of the church of Thyatira. The others have been warned through the prophecies of John and their remnants of this age refuse to repent. The angels of those churches have been removed. They no longer have a covering."

"I am sorry to hear that."

"The earth will experience a wickedness as never seen as the day of the Lord approaches. I have remitted various warnings for them to repent of their depravity and as a sign of the times. I opened the first four seals releasing deception, war, famine, and pestilence. They did not heed the warning. As you know, the fifth seal commences the tribulation while the sixth seal concludes it. The seventh seal activates judgment; for all will be judged according to their works. Before long, the fifth seal will be opened. Your mission has to be accomplished before I open the fifth seal."

"I understand my Lord. My assignment is of great importance."

The Son placed his hand on Michael's shoulder, "If you fail, the book of Revelation will be rewritten and The Adversary will accomplish his mission."

"That won't happen."

He handed Michael the sacred ancient silver rod, "Your wish has been granted. Your many millenniums as an archangel and your love for humankind make you perfect for this assignment. When the time is right, prepare for battle."

Michael held the rod with great authority as he illuminated with much strength and beauty. "I will not disappoint you."

CHAPTER FIFTEEN

Jensen stood in his boxers in front of his dresser with a huge smile on his face as he opened his dresser drawer to find a pair of pants and a shirt before he took a shower. His round belly slightly hung over his boxer shorts. He glanced in his floor model mirror as he tried to hold his stomach in. He said to himself aloud, "I'll be cool if I get rid of this gut". He scratched the nape of his short, curly strawberry blonde hair then rubbed his hairless chin. He thought to himself, *some facial hair would be nice too.* He reached into his drawer and pulled out a pair of black denim jeans. His bedroom door burst open, flew off the hinges, and hit the wall with a loud crash; denting the wall with the door knob. Pastor Jones stood in the doorway in a complete fit of rage.

Jensen's body tensed, he dropped his pair of jeans, as he exclaimed, "You scared the life out of me."

Pastor Jones walked in the room towards Jensen, combatively, "Did I? You should be afraid."

Pastor Jones gripped Jensen by his shoulders and hurled him onto the bed. Jensen bounced off the bed onto the floor as Pastor Jones soared on top of him, let a loose a ferocious, thunderous lion's roar, while his pupils transformed into slits exposing snake eyes. Jensen's entire body trembled in immeasurable fear.

"You were supposed to get close to her in order for her to trust you but not that close," Pastor Jones snarled.

"You promised me women and you didn't deliver." Jensen uneasily bellowed.

He snatched the collar of Jensen's shirt placing his face forehead to forehead with his. He threatened, "You idiot. She is mine. She will never want you, like you, nevertheless love you. She is incapable of loving anything or anyone other than herself. More than likely she is so disgusted with herself she does not want to be bothered with you. If she stays away from you, it ruins everything. Now I have to reevaluate my plan. You put a spell on her. Remove it now." Pastor Jones tossed Jensen across the bedroom.

Jensen took in a deep, hard swallow, as he landed on his bottom then mumbled, "I love her."

Pastor Jones released a ripping, bone chilling scream of fury that shattered the glass of Jensen's bedroom windows as in an explosion. He picked Jensen up from the floor by his chin and squeezed his chin slowly fracturing the bones until tears were released from Jensen's eyes. He threw Jensen against the wall with so much force he put a large dent into the wall. Jensen howled in pain as he slid to the floor in a sitting position.

"Is this how you treat the one who has given you so many gifts? She is mine. You cannot and will not *ever* have her. I will remove all the demons that dwell within you and take away all of your gifts. Your days of high priest are over. I will torture you, and when I am done, send you to hell to be tortured for all of eternity."

"Please don't. I'm sorry. I didn't know. I swear to you I didn't know. I don't want her. I don't please. How can I make amends? I'll do anything," Jensen cried.

"If you desire forgiveness and mercy, you should have given your allegiance to God."

"I will do anything, anything. Tell me what to do and I will do it. I can't feel my arms," Jensen bellowed.

Pastor Jones smirked, "Anything?...Michael, the archangel, is here in human form. I need you to lead him to me by taking something he desires. Remember to keep your eyes concealed because he can clearly see the ones who dwell within you through the windows of your soul."

Tears fell from Jensen's eyes, "I am no match for an archangel. Please give me another assignment. One that is more achievable. That is a job better fit for you. No one is more powerful than you. You created the earth and everything in it. You blessed us with the gift of wisdom."

While perched on the corner of Jensen's dresser, Pastor Jones teased, "Aw… The weeping and the whining…boo hew…boo hew. Such emotional creatures," He paused then said, "If I do it, it will certainly be hell on earth and we certainly do not want that until the appointed time. I have a feeling why Michael is here. As for the women, if you are that stimulated, have fun when you seize her for me," He smiled, "Now that I think about it I might put her aside for myself. There is nothing more gratifying than the defilement of a true believer. The very thought gives me wood."

Jensen's eyes grimaced, "What?"

"I don't sense her presence. Where is she?"

"She left, and I don't know where she went. The spell will be removed as soon as I get into the basement."

"It better."

"So, what's the plan?"

Three demons appeared in Jensen's bedroom standing near Pastor Jones. They slowly encircled Jensen.

Pastor Jones said, "Your friends will tell you everything and will lead the way. Remember, do not kill him by any means even if it places your life in jeopardy," While pointing to Zest, "You remember Zest do you not from contact through the board?"

"I remember Zest," Jensen said as he took a step back.

"If you fail, you will have to deal with me. Remember your curse. We have only one chance. Do not develop any ideas. Nothing can rid me from your life. You are in too deep. By the way, I need you to dispose of Nathan," Pastor Jones said while he dismounted from the dresser.

"Why me?"

"Must I do everything myself?" Pastor Jones stated then continued, "I need him out of my way. It's your choice. You have 72 hours."

Pastor Jones leisurely strode out of the room.

CHAPTER SIXTEEN

Jordin sat at her desk peering at Sonya's seemingly lifeless, dreaming body as her eyes pierced the dark corners of Sonya's soul, and her arched eyebrows grimaced something fierce. Her arms were folded across her chest as she took slow fierce breaths. She couldn't understand what was wrong with Sonya because she hadn't been home in nearly a week. In class, Sonya sat away from her and Adriana and left before they could speak to her about it. Normally she would call to let Jordin know what her plans were to prevent her from worrying. Now, she would leave and not say a word; stayed gone leaving Jordin to worry half to death about her.

Sonya didn't tell Jordin about her grandmother's medical mishap, and she found out through Ayana that Granna Nathan was within her last days. Usually Jordin would be the first to know and the first to lend a shoulder and an ear. Ever since that day at the library, Sonya didn't seem to want to be bothered with her anymore. Jordin yearned to talk to Sonya. She decided to watch her sleep, so when she awakened, the conversation couldn't be avoided, even if it meant missing her first class.

Sonya laid in her bed in a peaceful sleep, nettled on her side loosely tucked under the sheets, with her hair spread wildly, only revealing a small outline of her face. Sonya's body shuddered in response to the surrealism of her mind. She was dreaming dreams again:

Sonya stood in her pajamas and slippers on the Holy Mount in Zion, and saw seven angels holding the last seven plagues of God's wrath. She looked to her left and saw a sea of glass mixed with fire; standing to the right of her, near the sea of glass were multitudes upon multitudes of people holding harps. An angel of the Lord handed a harp to Sonya. The multitude of people sang the song of Moses the servant of God and the song of the Lamb: "Great and marvelous are your deeds, Lord God Almighty. Just and true are your ways, King of the ages. Who will not fear you, O Lord, and bring glory to your name? For you alone are holy. All nations will come and worship before you, for your righteous acts have been revealed."

She flew away and landed on a tall mountain as Elijah pointed to the sky, peering up at heaven while it stood open. As heaven opened, a rider on a white horse headed down whose name was Faithful and true, with eyes like blazing fire, and he had many crowns on his head. He was dressed in a robe that had been dipped in blood and his name was the Word of God. Then Elijah pointed down to the earth and Sonya saw a beast come up from the abyss with two horns like a lamb, but he spoke like a great dragon. He exercised all the authority of the first beast, whose fatal wound had healed, and this beast had the face of Pastor Jones.

Sonya awakened immediately with sweat beaded along her forehead and nose, her shirt stuck to her moist flesh, as her body glistened in the early morning light of the dorm room. Her heart rate excelled as she stared blankly. She turned her head to her desk and noticed Jordin sat with her arms crossed, her nose flared, and lips pinched tightly together. Sonya sat up in her bed and combed her hair with her fingers. She wiped the sweat from her nose and forehead with the palm of her hand and prepared. She knew Jordin was about to let her have it.

Jordin stared at Sonya as she unfolded her arms, "You awake yet?"

Sonya sighed. She rubbed her eyes with the palm of her hands, "Go ahead." She slid to the edge of the bed and rested her feet on the tan tiled floor; cold.

"What's goin' on with you? Why didn't you tell me about Granna Nathan?"

"Didn't think you'd care," Sonya stated as she slipped her feet into her pink furry slippers.

"What? You can't be serious." Jordin stated as she shook her head in disapproval. "This about the library ain't it?"

"Should it be?" Sonya said as she sat at her desk across from Jordin.

"You tell me."

Sonya rubbed the sleep crumbs from the corner of her eyes, "I needed to be alone. I'm trying to understand all of this."

"If you need to be alone, then say that. Don't shut me out. I was here losin' my brain cells lookin' for you and worried about you. Don't you ever do that to me again."

Sonya paused. She noticed the seriousness in Jordin's face and the sadness in her voice, "I'm sorry. It won't happen again. I was wrong for making you worry unnecessarily."

Jordin crossed her arms, "So tell me what's real. You pissed caused of the library?"

Sonya stared at the desk, "Pissed no. I admit it hurt for you of all people to abandon me like that." She stared in Jordin's eyes ensuring she clearly saw her emotions. "Adriana is expected because she's always been more your friend than mine. But you? It hurt. It truly hurt. Don't *you* do that to me again."

Jordin quickly rubbed her hair with her hand, "I was scared, okay? I ain't never been through nothin' like that in my life. You can't be tellin' people demons are behind me like that. You have to creep that up on somebody. I knew with your faith you would be okay. I left you because I knew out of anybody you were safe."

Sonya shook her head in disapproval, "How do you know that? What if I wasn't safe?"

"Because, unlike us you got God on your side."

"Wrong! Adriana has God on her side. She's the fucking saint. I'm far from one."

"What makes her a saint and not you? Both of you bitches are still virgins."

"Hmm. Just leave it alone alright."

"I saw that man Michael you've been dreaming about."

Sonya scratched her head, "What happened?"

"Nothing really. He just talked to me. He claims to be an angel."

"Do you believe him?"

"In a strange way, I do. There's something about him that's just so damn pure. You know I'm standoffish with strangers 'cuz I don't trust most people, but I felt so comfortable with him."

"I'll have to see for myself. Not to be funny but you're not the best judge of character."

"Please, you even said yourself that he's an angel in your dreams now you're doubting? Unbelievable."

"Well, why was he watching you?"

"He was keeping watch to protect me." Jordin giggled, "I have a real life angel watching my back. Isn't that something?...Yeah, he told me he really needs to speak with you as soon as possible. I told him he could come here and talk to you."

Sonya had a confused expression on her face, "I can't believe you did that. What does he want with me? I don't know Jordin. The bible doesn't say anything about things like this. How can you be so sure he's telling the truth about anything?"

"Trust me. He is telling the truth."

KENERLY PRESENTS

CHAPTER SEVENTEEN

Michael walked down the street near the old funeral home on his way to Jordin's dorm to speak with Sonya. The house seemed to watch Michael as he walked by. He stopped and took a long thorough look at it. The large white house trimmed in grey had large tented windows on the first floor with the entrance to the far left from where he stood. The first story looked like an office building. The second story of the house reminded him of a side profile of a mini castle. The roof seemed to be a collage of different shaped and sized triangles. He saw an unclean spirit peering out of the third story window at him. Michael heard doors slamming from within the house repeatedly, heard whispers, and turned his head in the direction of the sound. A fallen angel stood beside the large tree adjacent to the house then dissipated.

The wind went to war with his body sending chills down his spine making it difficult for him to adjust to the rotating temperatures, fluctuating between 36 and 5 degrees. Because of the frostiness of the Midwestern atmosphere, he yearned for the spring equinox, and his reaction to the temperature made him aware that his time was slim.

He walked along noticing fallen angels walking about; especially in the yard of the funeral home. Some of the fallen angels halted in their tracks upon sight of Michael. Some ran away and hid on sight while others aggressively proceeded towards him as Michael shook his head in disapproval. He did not feel up to a conflict. He simply wanted to speak with Sonya.

He approached a middle aged man walking by in the darkness of the early morning hours. He had an unshaved beard, chocolate complexion, and a baseball hat on his head, in his work clothes. He carried a crumbled brown paper bag that his lunch must have been in. He walked by, "Hey man."

"Hey," Michael stated in return. The man continued on down the street.

A high ranking fallen angel, Zest transcended from the man as he continued walking by. Zest stood in front of Michael with his shoulders square and fists clinched; pulsating. Michael could feel the immense hatred radiating from within him to the point of near suffocation. By Zest's courage and hatred, Michael knew he was in the presence of a high ranking fallen angel, and soon realized the reason the Father sent him to the Midwest, because it was the most haunted area of the United States. It made perfect sense for the Midwest to be haunted because the guardians lived here.

Michael reached inside of his trench coat and pulled out an ancient antiqued silver rod about seven inches in length. He gave it a forceful shake as two flaming blades, one on each end of the rod, emerged. Five demons, Causas, Fae, Azaric, Ahzrha, and Benz, joined Zest in a combative stance. All of them humanoid but appeared as dark, shadowy silhouettes.

Michael said, "No quarrel with you."

Zest snarled, "Why have you breached our kingdom?"

"I have not breached anything. I am here on my own accord. As soon as I am done, I will gladly leave this place," Michael said as he attempted to walk passed Zest.

Zest stuck his hand out onto Michael's chest to stop him. Michael gripped the rod prepared to attack if necessary.

Zest noticed the rod and quickly asked, "Are you in search of darkness? The Adversary told us you might come for her."

Michael's muscles flinched and Zest quickly removed his hand from upon his chest. Michael glanced at his distant fallen brothers in the distance, "I don't want any part to any darkness. The Adversary can have her if he wishes."

"You're up to something."

"You're up to something." Michael stated as he stared fearlessly into Zest's eyes. "No tricks or deception. I'm on my own accord. I will be gone within a very short space."

Michael looked across the street. A gang of demons, thirteen, come out from beyond the shadows. Michael stepped back and gripped the rod.

Zest smiled, "You are outnumbered. It's best you explain your purpose."

"It is best you let me by. You cannot harm me, but I can harm you." Michael stated.

Michael and Zest stared at each other for a few seconds in silence. Zest turned his head and peered up the street. A young man, 24 years old, walked down the opposite side of the street. He had a short haircut, barely there facial hair, caramel complexion, heavyset, with the appearance of a thug; the way his pants hung from his bottom. He smoked a cigarette and limped as he walked; holding his pants with one hand.

Zest turned and ran across the street. He slid inside of the young man. Michael shook his rod as the blades receded because the blades were ineffective for humans. He slid the rod into the inside pocket of his trench coat and continued up the street. The young man crossed the street towards him malevolently.

Michael stopped and stared at the young man. The young man's eyes transformed from a dark brown to a cold black as Zest controlled his body and pulled a 9mm hand gun from his jeans. Michael sighed. The young man shot at Michael; the sound of the shots echoed the silence of the early morning.

Michael ran toward a parked car as the young man released another shot; pop. A bullet grazed Michael's shoulder as he dove behind the car to shield himself. The young man approached the car with the gun pointed.

Michael crawled to the side of the car. His hands glowed brilliantly as he pulled the handle, opening the locked car door. He climbed into the driver seat as Zest, through the young man, took a shot at him. The bullet missed exiting the back windshield from the front windshield; piercing the glass. The young man took another shot from the front passenger side of the car. The bullet entered the windshield at an angle and pierced Michael's shoulder slinging him back into the seat. Michael's hands illuminated as he put the car in drive and drove off.

The young man shot at Michael again as the car drove by and pierced the same shoulder. Michael swerved almost hitting a parked car but continued up the street.

The young man returned his gun to his jeans. Zest snarled through him, "Just what I thought."

CHAPTER EIGHTEEN

Pastor Jones sat in his den behind his marble top cherry wood desk searching through a pile of papers. He searched thoroughly through the baptism records. He grabbed the baptism record for Adriana. She was a member of Jones' Temple for three years and was baptized three years ago, but now attended Precious Blood Cathedral. He held the record in his hand, crumbled it, and threw it into the small metal trash can next to his desk. He stared at the trashcan and it ignited. He allowed it to burn for 10 seconds then extinguished the flame with a quick stare. He sighed then ravished through the pile searching for a baptism record for Jordin. He searched and searched but didn't find one. Zest appeared from the dim corner of the room. Short, 5'7" inch humanoid, lean, with large hands and feet for his height and frame. Pastor Jones glanced up malevolently. "What?"

"Michael. I shot him. He's almost human." Zest responded as he approached Pastor Jones.

"Good", Pastor Jones stated as he stared at the metal trashcan and extinguished the flames.

"A few days ago saw him leaving the park with them." Zest enlightened.

"Them?" Pastor Jones stated. "Mmm…Jordin's with him…I don't recall seeing her…That doesn't make any sense. You were to scare her and keep her away from him." Pastor Jones knocked the pile of papers onto the floor and leaned back in his chair; scowling.

"I tried. Seems Sonya is her best friend."

Pastor Jones stared at Zest then rubbed his chin. "I know. That is why I have been keeping a watch on her." He said to himself aloud. "You must get them away from each other, and most importantly keep them away from him.

"Why? Wouldn't it be best to wait until we find out his purpose? We could use Jordin as bait to bring him to us." Zest proposed.

Pastor Jones stood and walked towards the window. He peered out and placed his hand against the glass. "No. I have another plan. Sonya's visions are important prophecy. I need her with me. That is why I am in the process of establishing trust."

Mrs. Jones yelled from the other room, "William…Have you prepared the sermon for the youth ministry program?'

Pastor Jones exhaled rapidly, "That woman." Pastor Jones walked towards the doorway and yelled out of the open door, "No. How many times do I have to tell you that?"

Zest smirked, "What is your plan? Where do I come in?"

"You possessed that woman who chased Jordin, right?"

"Yes."

"You were at the library, right?"

"Yes."

"You possessed Jensen, right?"

"Yes."

"I don't need you to do anything because you failed. You failed at everything I instructed you to do." Pastor Jones stated as he walked towards Zest.

"I tried. Michael interfered and Sonya prayed…"

Pastor Jones kicked the desk denting the dark oak wood, "I can't stand to hear his name!" Pastor Jones snarled in an inhumane voice.

"What was that honey," Mrs. Jones said as she approached the doorway and walked in.

Pastor Jones glared at her malevolently, "I wasn't talking to you."

"Oh, well I'm heading to moms. Are you joining me?"

"No."

Mrs. Jones paused then said, "Okay, well I'll bring you a plate." She walked away.

Pastor Jones turned to Zest, "Beliah."

"What about him?"

"He is trying to help them." Pastor Jones said as he walked to the window and opened it.

"Help them do what?"

"Save their souls. I want you to follow Sonya, frighten her to near death, and take something away from her." Pastor Jones peered out of the window. "Jordin is already mine."

"Adriana?"

"She is quite the prize. Leave her be for the moment. I have a special plan for her."

"What about Michael?"

"Let him do him. I think I have an idea why he's here thanks to Sonya. As for Beliah, I will take care of him." Pastor Jones smirked.

"What about Pastor Ryan?"

Pastor Jones smirked, "The pieces are already on the board. A few more moves then checkmate."

CHAPTER NINETEEN

Jensen knelt in front of an Ankh symbol resting on the wall trying to conjure up the Egyptian goddess Isis. Directly below the Ankh was a goat head, the symbol of Baphomet hanging on the wall. He knelt inside of an inverted pentagram, painted on his basement floor in human blood from the many sacrifices he made to the Goddess, Baal, Molech, and The Adversary himself. Four corners of the encircled inverted pentagram had lighted candles. Under the head of Baphomet was a Thaumaturgic Triangle painted in dried blood with human hair attached to it. He grabbed a hold of the charm on his necklace; a Satanic Cross, represented by an upside down question mark, with a cross at the end, representing the three crowned princes of the underworld. He grabbed a handful of small crystals out of a silver inscribed bowl and rested them within the palms of his hands. He closed his eyes and mumbled in another tongue.

Jensen mumbled as he closed his hands around the crystals and brought his hands together. His hands rested before him knuckle to knuckle and thumb to thumb. The lights of the candles flickered repeatedly. Jensen continued with his séance. He lifted his closed fists above his head still knuckle to knuckle and thumb to thumb. He pulled his hands apart forming a "v" formation above his head. His eyes rolled in the back of his head as he opened his hands, palms facing the ceiling, as some of the crystal slid between his spread fingers approached the floor. The crystals did not touch the floor; they hovered an inch above it and danced. The Thaumaturgic Triangle opened as Beliah stepped out of it. As soon as he stepped out of the doorway between the supernatural realm and the physical realm, the triangle closed and the crystals plummeted to the floor. Jensen's eyes rolled forward.

Beliah stood nine feet tall scraping his head against the basement ceiling. He was embodied in a crimson colored light and his features were humanoid; having the face of a man. He was athletic built appearing to be a heavy weight boxer with raw sienna colored eyes.

Jensen's eyes bellowed and his mouth opened wide as he witnessed this enormous fallen angel. He knew he made a huge mistake because he desired to conjure the goddess. Out of fear, Jensen bowed to him.

Beliah scowled, "Get up."

Jensen stood and faced Beliah.

Beliah stared down at him, "Why did you summon me?"

"I didn't. I summoned the goddess Isis because I needed her advice and maybe her help. I don't know what happened," Jensen stated as his hands danced uncontrollably.

"Isis?" Beliah smirked, "You mean Leviathan?

"I...I..."

"Mmm. What do want from me?" Beliah asked as he drew near.

Jenson stepped backwards knocking over one of his candles, "Can you advise me?"

Beliah rubbed his chin, "I'm listening."

Jensen picked up the candle and stood it upright. He paced back and forth glancing at Beliah and glancing away, "Satan deceived you into falling. You have animosity towards him, right?"

Beliah giggled, "Is that what you think? Ignorance kills the ability to reason."

Jenson appeared confused. He stared at Beliah as Beliah crossed his arms. Beliah sat on the table, "Continue." He pierced Jensen with his eyes.

"I did something to piss him off. I know he's going to kill me."

Beliah clinched his hands together, "So where do I come in?"

"I know who darkness is and I need you to help me keep him away from her. If he can't get darkness, he can't initiate his plan."

Beliah laughed at Jensen, "Your plan is foolish. How stupid do you think he is? He already knows you contacted me because his legions are loyal to him. The ones who dwell within you will tell him what you're up to."

Terror struck Jensen's face, "So what do I do?"

"Give your allegiance to God. It is not too late for you. The Adversary is going to torture you to death but at least you can save your soul."

Jensen mugged, "If it's that easy, why don't you do it?"

"We have full understanding and knowledge of the Father and his ways. We don't get second chances, but you do, because you do not have full understanding and knowledge. We left on our own freewill while your kind was removed as punishment for sin. Being removed as punishment makes you redeemable. Leaving, willful disobedience is not tolerated. The Father is a merciful, forgiving God for your kind. If you turn to him, he will accept you. However, it won't prevent you from being tortured or dying in your flesh."

Jensen's face turned red, "God is not just and true. He kept us in ignorance. He didn't give Lucifer a chance or you. The Adversary opened our eyes and gave us wisdom…"

Beliah interrupted, "Stop entertaining those lies. Lucifer gave you the wisdom to be like him, a desire to be like God. To this very day, your kind yearns to be your own gods. Telling yourselves that you are little gods. It's the very idea that resulted in our banishment in the first place. He has led you astray since the creation."

Jenson frowned, "Why should I believe you? You are weak."

Beliah illuminated expressing his rage. "You are foolish, ignorant, and stupid! We are of much higher wisdom, much higher intellect than your kind and he deceived us. You think he can't deceive you? The very thought of you trying to outthink us is ridiculous; especially if you think you can outthink him."

Jensen swallowed deeply. He walked away from Beliah, "You are pathetic; a traitor to your kind… I have less than 12 hours. You can go back the way you came."

Beliah shook his head in disapproval, "You don't listen. As soon as you hear something you don't agree with, you close your ears, your mind, and your hearts. Humanity? I get it now. Now I clearly see. Your race is infantile, arrogant, ignorant, egotistic, and proud. Our purpose was not to bow down to you. Our purpose was to guide you," Beliah snickered while shaking his head in disappointment, "If I knew then, what I know now I would not have fallen. Something in the core of my being told me not to, but I didn't listen. You have a chance for redemption instead you choose this? You deny paradise for hell?"

"Hell doesn't exist or else you'd be there now," Jensen arrogantly stated.

Beliah grabbed a hold of Jensen and pulled him near. He clinched his head with his large hand as his hands illuminated. He reached inside of Jensen and snatched his soul from his body. Beliah stared at Jensen's soul and hurled him into hell:

Jensen fell down a dark shaft as his body tumbled uncontrollably in the air, and his arms frantically reached out to grab a hold of anything to prevent him from falling. While plummeting swiftly down the shaft, the odor became more and more concentrated; the worse smell he had ever smelled in his entire life. It was a combination of trash, underarms, rotten meat, rotten cheese, and bad breath. The closer he got to the bottom of the shaft the hotter it became as sweat beaded on his forehead and nose. He continued down the shaft for another two minutes.

Jensen smacked the bottom of the shaft and struck the floor on his stomach; he searched around the extremely hot room, noticed he was in a prison cell similar to that of ancient times, with walls of stones and metal bars. Unlike modern prison cells, there wasn't a bed, sink, or bathroom in the room. He stood to his feet in tremendous pain from the fall, realizing he was completely naked, and covered his genitals with his hands to shield his nakedness.

The odor he smelled along the fall had intensified by the hundred – thousands, and was so horrendous, he tried to hold his breath, so he didn't have to smell it, but it did no good. He heard breathing sounds around him and felt the presence of others in the cell. He had never felt so much evil in his life and soon realized there were three beasts in the cell with him. Jensen shouted, "Who is there?"

One beast snarled, "I smell a human."

The second beast said, "Hate them, hate them, hate them."

The third beast drew near, "Why are you here? You…You…You!"

The third beast snatched Jensen by the crown of his head, as he was weightless to him, and hurled him into the wall. He struck the wall with an immeasurable amount of force then he slid onto the dusty, hot floor on his stomach. He felt so much impenetrable pain that he couldn't move. The amount of pain he experienced seemed illusory but was real. The second beast drew near him and stomped on his back and held his foot there smashing him. It felt, as though, he was trapped under a semi-truck. He suffocated as the pain caused him to yearn for death. The beast removed his foot from Jensen's back, and walked towards the wall, beating his chest in fury and resentment.

After about two minutes, Jensen recovered a little energy as he screamed for help. No one came to his rescue. A voice shouted, "Time!" As the prison door opened, the beasts walked out. Jensen laid there for several minutes then got up and walked out of the cell.

It was pitch black as he walked sightlessly in the darkness and immediately plunged down another shaft. The only light he caught sight of was blue and white flickering lights. He bellowed in terror as he dropped down the shaft, tumbling uncontrollably, reaching his arms out again to grab a hold of anything to prevent him from falling. As he momentary searched his surroundings, he noticed Adriana and Ayana falling down the shaft alongside him. They cried and screamed with expressions of horror on their faces.

When they spattered the bottom of the shaft, they were in a lake of fire. The fire was so hot the flames were white. Jensen observed the flesh melt off of Adriana and Ayana then regenerated to burn off again. Jensen was in the lake of fire with them and felt every inch of the scolding from the flames. His flesh melted as the heat was reminiscent to the temperature of the sun magnified by 50,000. He heard an earsplitting lion's roar and wild animal sounds that echoed in his ears.

Jensen's soul returned to his body with a deep breath as Beliah still held him off his feet by the crown of his head. He had only been gone for a few seconds. Jensen screamed and screamed something terrible. Beliah dropped him to the floor as he landed on his side. Jensen continued screaming hysterically as he held himself close; body danced uncontrollably.

Beliah stated, "Hell doesn't exist?"

Jensen cried like a newborn infant and continued crying. Beliah peered down at him.

"The choice is yours. It is not too late. Give your allegiance to The Father." He vanished.

KENERLY PRESENTS

CHAPTER TWENTY

Pastor Ryan folded a large pile of clothes in the basement of the church, placing them in the three feet by two feet box with a width of eighteen inches. The basement was cold, dim, with the appearance typical of an unfinished basement that often leaked when it rained. The basement was silent and littered with boxes, some open, some closed, and some sealed with tape but all stacked neatly supplying ample walk room.

Pastor Ryan had a light pale complexion because in his younger days he was a red head, but these days, the hair on his head and face were white. At 85 years old, he was a chubby man with a round belly and full beard that put most people in the mind of Santa Claus. He had a really calm speaking voice and wore a navy blue "v" neck sweater with a tan button down shirt underneath. He always smiled and had this glow about him that drew people into him like a magnet. He certainly was a light in the dark for those who were hurting inside or just plain confused about life.

His wife washed these clothes because his congregation donated them to the homeless shelter every season. As he was folding the clothes and placing them into the box, the basement lights flickered. He paused looking up at the lights. They flickered again then dimmed. The hairs on the back of his neck stood as he could sense an insatiable amount of evil.

"In the name of the Father, the Son, and the Holy Spirit, I rebuke you. I rebuke you in the name of Jesus Christ! Get ye behind me Satan!" Pastor Ryan shouted.

"I'm not Satan, and I'm already behind you. Don't you know it takes more than a simple rebuke to get rid of me?" Pastor Jones said as he stood on the fourth step from the floor of the basement.

Pastor Ryan ran towards a shelf in the basement full of books and grabbed a bible as Pastor Jones calmly walked down the stairs. As soon as Pastor Ryan grabbed the bible, Pastor Jones released a shrieking lion's roar as the bible flew out of Pastor Ryan's hand.

Pastor Ryan turned to Pastor Jones and said, "In the name of Jesus Christ, I command you to leave him!"

Pastor Jones' hand trembled a bit as he walked towards Pastor Ryan, "There will be a great day when every knee will bow in regards to his name, and confess him with their mouths, but not today," He pointed towards himself, "He is mine. Always have been and always will be mine. I will kill him before I allow you to rid me of him."

"In Jesus' name, what do you want?" Pastor Ryan yelled.

"To kill you."

"In the name of Jesus, why do you want me dead?"

"So you cannot interfere more than you already have. Filling her head with righteousness and truth? But how much of what you said is actually true?," Pastor Jones said as he pulled an eight inch long knife out of his coat pocket.

"You can kill my body, but my spirit belongs to God. I don't fear you Abaddon. You think you're proving a point showing yourselves to people. Showing your demons to people to scare them. All you're doing is sending them to God. Once they realize demons are real, it assures them God and his Son are real."

Pastor Jones swung the knife at Pastor Ryan and sliced his hand, "You know nothing. My people have infiltrated churches, governments, government organizations, religious movements, and the list goes on. Your people prefer my mark over the seal of the Father. Soon, your kind will be extinguished as the inhabitants of the earth gloat and celebrate by sending each other presents," He giggled, "All the inhabitants of the earth will burn in hell with me."

Pastor Ryan's hand bled onto the floor, "You know scripture well. Since you know scripture, you should also know multitudes that no one can count from every nation, tribe, people and language will stand before the throne in front of the lamb from the great tribulation… You will lose."

"And I will enjoy bringing as many of them as I can with me," Pastor Jones said as he drew near Pastor Ryan.

Pastor Ryan ran towards the bookcase and grabbed a crucifix. He turned to Pastor Jones with the crucifix pointed towards him, "I bind you in the name of the Father, the Son, and the Holy Spirit. I command you to leave in the name of Jesus Christ. I do not fear you Abbadon."

"Who?" Pastor Jones calmly stated as he lifted Pastor Ryan off his feet with a stare.

Pastor Jones' eyes morphed to snake eyes as he growled like a ferocious wild lion then he hissed like a snake as his body swayed back and forth like a cobra. Terror struck the soul of Pastor Ryan upon seeing that. Pastor Jones paused, frozen, without moving a muscle. His irises turned a cold black as he stood frozen just staring at Pastor Ryan without blinking his eyes one time. Pastor Ryan took in a deep breath then took in a hard slow swallow. He had no idea what the possessed Pastor Jones was up to. Suddenly, Pastor Jones blinked, opened his mouth, and released an earsplitting lion's roar that shattered the glass of the basement windows. The sound was piercing as Pastor Ryan's ears bled and he grabbed his ears and closed his eyes. With a glance, he hurled Pastor Ryan into the wall.

Pastor Ryan's shoulder popped out of place as he slid to the floor. He moaned in tremendous pains. Pastor Jones appeared on top of him with saliva dribbling from his mouth.

Pastor Ryan's eyes narrowed, "You have lost."

Pastor Jones snarled as he backed up and stood in front of Pastor Ryan. He ripped his shirt off as wings burst out of Pastor Jones' shoulder blades. The Adversary stepped out of Pastor Jones' body as Pastor Jones, imperceptibly, crumbled to the floor.

The Adversary stood embodied in a beautiful light. His appearance was humanoid as he was athletic built, light beige complexion, with long silky, wavy blonde hair. His eyes were a deep blue like that of a sapphire, and his thick eyebrows accented his face well. He was a mighty man wearing an off white robe without a sash of precious stones. He stood so tall he had to bend his head down.

Pastor Ryan was astounded. He couldn't believe how beautiful The Adversary was. The Adversary knelt before Pastor Ryan, "Do you know what today is?"

"Monday," Pastor Ryan stated as he glanced at his bible on the floor about five feet away from him.

"My favorite day of the week. It's also the 11th; one of my favorite numbers and is the number of my name. You think you know me pastor. You know nothing."

"What's the point of this? You can't kill a true believer without God's permission. You cannot kill me." Pastor Ryan screamed as sweat glistened on his forehead.

"Sadly you have mistaken. Seems you have misunderstood the Book of Job. Again, you know nothing." The Adversary stared at Pastor Jones.

"Lies. There is no truth in you," Pastor Ryan bellowed in pain.

The Adversary blew his finger nail, "Normally, you would be correct...For the sake of your shame. I will not dispatch you. I will have your former student do it. 'A student is not above his teacher, nor a servant above his master.' I reprove this. Today, the student is greater than his teacher."

Pastor Jones stared blankly. The Adversary telepathically said, "Dispatch him or I will dispatch you."

Pastor Jones picked up the knife and stood. He clinched it securely as he closed his eyes and took a hard swallow. He did not want to murder his former teacher or anyone else, but he feared The Adversary; even more he feared an early death. He walked towards Pastor Ryan as Pastor Ryan stared him in his eyes; unafraid.

Pastor Ryan stood facing him, "The Lord is my Shepherd; I shall not want. He maketh me lie down in the green pastures..."

The Adversary interrupted, "He leadeth you beside the still waters. He restoreth your soul…blah, blah, blah…hurry up. He annoys me."

Pastor Jones stared at Pastor Ryan in admiration because he was not afraid. He took in a slow, deep, hard swallow then glanced at The Adversary. The Adversary stood with his arms folded across his chest. Pastor Jones closed his eyes and blindly swung the knife slashing Pastor Ryan's throat. Pastor Ryan gargled the blood for a few seconds then dropped to the floor. Pastor Jones dropped the knife while keeping his eyes closed tightly.

CHAPTER TWENTY ONE

Michael pulled up and parked the car he stole across the street from the ice cream shop in front of an abandoned car dealership. He opened the door and slowly climbed out. He touched his shoulder as his face frowned. He was in tremendous pain from the two gunshot wounds, but since he was only half human, the bleeding had stopped and the wounds were healing at an alarming rate. He closed the car door and rubbed his hands together. It was quite frigid that morning as he could see his breath every time he exhaled. There was no heat in the abandoned building he stayed in, so he looked around for a place he could get warm. He noticed the ice cream shop down the street on the corner. As he walked across the street towards the ice cream shop, he saw Sonya walk in. He sped up the pace so he could catch up to her without running because he didn't want to frighten her.

Sonya stood across from the order counter trying to figure out what she wanted. She couldn't decide between the cookies and cream, banana split, or strawberry shortcake. She gazed at the overhead menu indecisively. She unzipped her grey pea coat to give her body some breathing room. The temperature was on hell as her forehead shined. She patted her dark denim jean pockets trying to remember if she grabbed the change from her desk.

The cashier said, "May I help you?"

"I'm undecided right now," Sonya said as she backed away from the counter while piercing the menu.

Michael approached her from behind and whispered, "May I suggest the strawberry shortcake?"

Sonya turned to him and did a double take as her mouth dropped and her eyes bulged. Michael stood six feet two inches tall, athletic build, with the most gorgeous smile she had ever seen. He didn't have a stitch of facial hair, but his almond shaped eyes were outlined with long curly eyelashes as his eyes seemed to sparkle. He was exceptionally neat and clean, with a blue button down shirt, a nice pair of denim jeans, and a trench coat. At five feet two inches tall, Michael seemed like a giant compared to her.

Michael smiled and extended his hand, "I'm Michael."

Sonya took a step backwards and shook his hand as she inhaled his cologne; reminiscent of a love potion. She was hypnotized by his smile as she gazed at him feeling at peace holding onto his hand.

Michael nodded his head as his deep voice asked, "May I have my hand back, please?"

Sonya snapped back into reality, "Sonya, I'm Sonya." She quickly released his hand with a hint of embarrassment.

Michael said, "Faithful and true."

Sonya raised one thinly arched eyebrow, "You must be a Christian?"

Michael quickly blurted as he placed his hands into his coat pocket, "No. I am not a Christian, but I know God well." Michael chuckled as Sonya smiled.

Sonya looked at Michael and blushed, "I guess I'll take your word for it." She turned to the cashier. "I'd like a strawberry shortcake please."

The cashier rung up her order and said, "That'll be $4.39. Would you like anything else?"

Sonya reached into her purse, "No that will be all. Thank you." She pulled out her wallet, grabbed a $5 bill, and handed it to him. He quickly handed her the change. Sonya tossed the change into her purse and zipped it.

Michael stared at Sonya dreamily. He said, "Would you like to sit?"

Sonya smiled, "Sure."

Michael led Sonya to the booth where he sat. They sat down across from each other as Sonya slid her coat off and placed her purse on top of the table.

Michael picked up his coffee and took a sip.

Sonya glanced at him and smiled. She looked away then did it again.

Michael smirked, "What?"

"This may sound strange but I saw you in my dreams...I saw you at the library. Why didn't you help me?" Sonya pulled her hair behind her ears and scratched her ear.

"I don't know what you're talking about. I was never at a library. I can assure you." Michael leaned back.

Sonya examined Michael with her eyes. She looked at his full silky lips that were shaped like a cupid's bow. She stared into his big dark brown eyes, "I promise I saw you at the library while I was being attacked."

"I promise you that it was not me. I was not ever at any library."

The cashier yelled, "Strawberry shortcake."

"Already?" Sonya stood, "I'll be right back." She walked to the counter. Michael nodded in approval.

Michael watched her walk away. He stared at her bright white silhouette admiring the view because he could clearly see the Holy Spirit in her. He sighed. She was the first true believer he met since transcending to earth. When Sonya turned around on her way back, he redirected his attention.

Sonya sat down with the large strawberry shortcake. The aroma of the fresh strawberries overwhelmed Michael's heavenly scent, "Wow.

I didn't know it would be so big. I don't think I could eat all of this by myself and I'd hate to waste."

Michael took a sip of his coffee, "Eat what you can. Trust me, you will not be disappointed."

Sonya took a bite of her strawberry shortcake, "Mm. You're right. This is good. It's really good."

Michael smiled, "Told you so."

"If you weren't outside of the library, who was?"

"I don't know. Evil spirits can mimic and portray themselves as anyone they choose."

Sonya said, "Hmmm…you're scaring me. So Michael. I've never seen you around here. Are you new in town?"

"Yes. I am, but I won't be here too much longer."

She picked at her dessert, "Why is that?"

"Well, once I'm done here, I have to go back home."

"Oh. So where do you stay? Anywhere around here?" Sonya took a bite of the strawberry shortcake, grabbed her head, and closed her eyes; cold too cold.

Michael smirked, "Yes. I stay near."

Sonya rubbed her temples and asked, "Apartment or a house?"

"The dark brown building right next door," Michael took a sip of his coffee.

Sonya took another bite of her strawberry shortcake, "Mm...Wow. I'm sorry. You seem so educated. I never would have suspected you to be homeless."

"Education has nothing to do with homelessness...This may seem strange, but I need your help."

Sonya looked up as her eyebrows grimaced, "My help? With what?"

Michael rubbed his head, "Your father is Richard Nathan, correct?"

"Yeah. How did you know?" She leaned back in her seat with one eyebrow raised, "So it's true, hunh? Jordin said you were an angel...in my dreams you're an angel. Well, most of the time. Sometimes you're a demon."

Michael rubbed his eye with his index finger, "A demon?" Michael chuckled then continued, "I assure you I'm an angel in search of ceremonial trumpets. Your family, the descendants of the Levites, has those trumpets. You've had them for millenniums upon millenniums."

Sonya leaned up with her elbows on the table, "Trumpets? So you've been following and basically stalking Jordin for some musical instruments that my family has? I've never seen any trumpets."

"They are much more than that. These trumpets are needed to summon the two witnesses of the tribulation. Without these witnesses, the heavenly signs of the sixth seal will not occur. Without these witnesses, there isn't anyone to preach the Word of God to the inhabitants of the earth. If I don't obtain those trumpets, no one other than true believers before the tribulation will be saved. The heavenly signs show people who God is. The two witnesses prepare the way for the seventh seal to be opened to begin the order of the trumpets and the seven woes leaving behind only those who have the mark of the beast to endure that judgment."

Sonya sat in silence. She leaned back in her seat as she crossed her arms, "You expect me to believe God has chosen me, little old me, out of everyone in this world, to help you; an angel, with a mission this grand, vital, and important?"

"That is exactly what I am saying."

"Why didn't he send you directly to my elders instead of me?"

"I have no idea. Look, the longer I stay in this flesh, the more human I become. I have lost half of my powers. I don't have much time before I am completely mortal. I need to speak with your father as soon as possible."

Sonya uncrossed her arms, "Now, I know I can be gullible and a bit naïve, but this takes the cake."

Michael reached across the table and grabbed her arm, "Please just listen."

Sonya snatched her arm away from him, "Stay away from me."

"Don't lose your faith now. This is what he wants you to do."

"My faith. What do you know about my faith? You want me to believe you're an angel? God doesn't intervene in this day and age. Jesus was the last intervention. Angels will not come to earth other than to sound the trumpets. I've read Revelation many times. Are you telling me the words in that book are a lie?"

"When you were six, you were diagnosed with bacterial meningitis. You were in the intensive care ward, and you knelt by the edge of your bed. You cried. I will never forget your prayer. You said, 'Dear God, if you are real, please don't let me die. My mom and dad would be really sad. They need me in their lives. Mom says I am the only good thing she's ever done. I'm the only thing she's ever been proud of. My mom cries when she thinks I am asleep. Can you make her happy again? Would you please wrap your arms around her to comfort her? If you're listening to me, please show me a sign.'"

Sonya's mouth opened wide. Michael grabbed her hand and continued, "I was there with you as your guardian angel. When you cried because God did not show you a sign, I held you and comforted you. Every time you prayed, you always asked for a sign and never received one. But you kept your faith anyway. You want a sign. I will give you one."

Sonya's cell phone rang. She picked it up and looked at the caller I.D. It was Sister Beth. Sonya answered, "Hello!"

"Sonya, I'm sorry to tell you, but Pastor Ryan is dead."

"What? I just saw him the other day and he was healthy. He was fine."

"Someone slashed his throat in the basement. Martha found him when she went down to get the clothes for the shelter. He was murdered. Only in this wicked world would someone shank a pastor."

Tears swelled in Sonya's eyes, "Oh my goodness...."

"Don't make no sense. How could anybody want to hurt a man of God? Good God fearing man. Mm. Mm. Lord...Gal, everybody is going to his house this evening to show our respects. I just thought you should know because you youngsters don't watch the news. A bomb could be heading our way and y'all wouldn't know it. I think it would be nice for Sherry to see you. It might make her feel a little better."

Sonya paused as her breathing slowed. She sighed as more tears swelled in her eyes, "Oh my...I...I... have to go." Sonya hung up the phone.

Michael stared at her as his eyes drooped. His heart went out to her as he felt her sadness in the core of his being. Sonya slowly laid her phone on the table as her nose flared and her chin quivered. She stared at the table.

"What is wrong?" Michael asked

"It was nice to meet you, but I have to go." Sonya put her coat on and grabbed her purse. She slid out of the booth without looking at him. Michael slid out of the booth behind her.

"Where can I find you? Where can I find your father?" Michael asked.

Sonya quickly exited the ice cream shop without responding to him. Michael stood frozen in silence. He stared up at the ceiling and mumbled, "You are not going to make this easy for me are you?" He ran out behind Sonya.

CHAPTER TWENTY TWO

Sonya briskly walked down the street with tear filled eyes refusing to cry. She walked away from the campus towards a nearby neighborhood. She didn't know where she was going because she was unfamiliar with the neighborhood she headed towards. She just needed to get away from everything and everyone so she could have time to herself to think and rationalize the entire situation.

She knew Michael told her the truth about being an angel, but it was so difficult for her to believe that she was chosen by The Father to help him with such a vital mission. She began to understand her dreams a little better as she thought back to what Pastor Jones said about her dreams being visions instead of simple dreams. Puzzled, she wondered why Pastor Jones was in her dream playing the trumpets Michael searched for. She thought to herself, *what's the deal with Pastor Jones?* He was mighty interested in her dreams, and every time she saw him, he always asked about them yet told her they were a manifestation of her own guilt. It seemed Pastor Jones contradicted his own words at times. Sonya also wondered why in some of her dreams Michael was a demon with fangs and roaring like a rabid beast. The conflicting dreams of a good and evil Michael also didn't make sense to her. Then she thought about Jordin. Jordin was terrified of him then even she had a change of heart after meeting him and didn't even believe in angels and demons at first.

As she walked, she saw a sign that read "Uriel's". It was posted as the name of a barber shop. Sonya thought back to the dream she had the night before:

Sonya awakened in a cold, dark basement. The only light was that of the moon that shone through a tiny window, the only window that was not boarded up. She could barely see through the darkness past 6 feet, and although she couldn't see, she knew someone was there with her. She called out, "Whose there?" No one said anything, but she heard heavy breathing. She slowly crept closer to the window where the light shone through. She said, "There's nothing to be afraid of. I won't hurt you. Who's there?" She heard a glass clink against the basement floor then the jar rolled towards her stopping two feet in front of her. A voice she recognized said, "You're in danger." Sonya took in a deep hard swallow. She said, "Show yourself." Pastor Jones calmly strode into the beam of the moon light with one hand in his dress pants pocket as though he was holding onto something. Sonya saw a bright white light flicker from the corner of her left eye. She turned her head in that direction. The light glowed brightly illuminating the entire basement. She saw the silhouette of a man as she shielded her eyes. She turned her head and Pastor Jones had vanished. Sonya said, "Who are you?" The bright silhouette muttered, "Uriel, an archangel of The Father; the Archangel of wisdom. When in trouble, you call for

*me and I will come. Trouble is surrounding you, but you
are never alone."*

Sonya remembered awakening feeling so happy and at peace. She sighed wishing life was always that peaceful. For the first time in months, her dreams were actually better than her reality.

Michael caught up to Sonya as she walked down the street. Sonya's stomach continuously cramped as they walked as though her intuition was warning her that she was heading in the wrong direction. She held her arm firm against her stomach as her face frowned a little. She wondered if maybe she ate the little bit of ice cream she did eat too fast or maybe it just didn't agree with her. Either way, she needed to excuse the negative feeling she felt in her soul because she didn't want to turn back and walk towards the campus.

Michael said, "Hey."

Sonya stopped then turned to him, "Look, you have to give me a minute. Someone just murdered my pastor and this is…a lot…guess this is why we're being chased and stalked by demons, hunh?"

"Maybe so, but I think they have their own plan."

"Trumpets? I had a dream about trumpets. Long silver trumpets without keys. "

"Those are it. Those are the trumpets I need. Do you know where they are?"

"No. If I knew, I would tell you and gladly give them to you so all of this would stop. It'd be nice to be able to sleep again."

Michael stopped in his tracks. He stared blankly into the air thinking. Sonya suddenly noticed everyone they passed seemed to stare at her, frown, and snarl. Sonya rubbed her eyes with her index fingers and ignored the passerby's. Michael stared at Sonya concerned, "You're frightened?"

Sonya placed her hands in her coat pocket, "Overwhelmed. I'm still trying to rationalize everything. Makes sense, but at the same time, doesn't make any sense. The dreams I've had about heaven isn't anything like I've been told. The only thing true is all angels are male."

Michael smirked, "Who told you that?"

"Every minister, pastor, and believer I've ever known."

"How can a human who has never been to heaven accurately describe heaven?"

"I don't know."

"Your kind will never have a home in the heavens. Your home is here. The kingdom will be established here. Heaven comes to earth and not the other way around."

"So once your mission is over, you go back?"

Michael smiled, "Of course. That is my home. That is where I belong."

"This can't be real. I'm walking down the street with an angel. Why you're the great archangel Michael."

Michael stopped in front of the entrance of a dead end alley, "I'm aware of how this all may seem and sound, but time is of the essence. I'm here for a very short space."

"So I'll help you then you'll abandon me. What happens to me when you leave?"

"You will be greatly blessed."

Sonya diverted her attention to the ground, "I mean will the haunting continue? Will it get worse?"

Michael said, "I don't know. I have no control over what they decide to do, but I assure you The Father will never leave you nor forsake you."

Sonya stared at the ground. Michael saw the sadness in her eyes as she silently doubted the security and extent of her safety once he left. He took his hand and placed it under her chin lifting her head up to look at him. He smiled, "I promise I will protect you…You know, people like you give me hope for the condition of humanity."

"I don't understand how. I'm a liar. I have everyone convinced that I'm still a virgin…plus some other things I've done in the past that I consider the unmentionable."

"Everyone falls short. You're human. You're not infallible." Michael glanced at his surroundings then continued, "I know this place." He stared down the dead end alley, pointed then continued, "This is where I came through the portal."

"Portal?"

"Yes. There's a sporting goods store down this way. We can get some supplies. Come on."

"Supplies?" Sonya mumbled.

Michael led Sonya down the dead end alley towards the Sporting Goods store.

Michael stood at the back door of the sporting goods store. He placed his hand on the locked door knob as his hand illuminated. He turned the knob and opened the door. He walked in as Sonya stood staring at him. Michael said, "What?"

"Isn't stealing a sin?"

Michael smiled, "You can wait here in 18 degree temperatures if you prefer."

Sonya smiled. Michael paused and looked around. Sonya's eyebrows frowned as she looked around, "What?"

Michael placed his finger vertically across his lips and said, "Shhh!" His eyes pierced their surroundings. He stepped away from the door towards the alley searching with his eyes. He reached inside of his trench coat and pulled out the ancient silver rod. He stood in front of Sonya shielding her, "I know you're here. Show yourself."

Molech said, "I don't take orders from anyone." The door to the sporting goods store slammed shut startling Sonya because she could hear the voice but could not see him and neither could Michael.

Baal said, "He who has not sinned cast the first stone."

Michael firmly gripped the silver rod, "I have no quarrel with you. We'll be leaving now."

Michael grabbed Sonya's hand and proceeded towards the street. Baal stepped out from behind the large dumpster and stood in front of them. He was 8 feet tall, humanoid, with a pair of three inch horns extending from his forehead. His fists balled tightly in a combative stance. Sonya clinched tightly to Michael's hand as she stepped behind him and whispered, "Who is that?"

Michael whispered, "Baal, the false god of fertility; A fallen one who desires to be worshipped like The Father. One of the false gods of ancient polytheism."

Molech materialized six feet behind Michael and Sonya. He was thirteen feet tall, humanoid, skin the color of burnt brass, and an athletic build. Michael shook the rod revealing the flaming blades. He turned sideways in between Molech and Baal so he could see the both of them. As soon as he let her hand loose, Sonya clinched onto the back of Michael's trench coat hanging on for dear life.

Sonya whispered, "Oh my god. Who is that?"

Michael whispered, "Molech, another fallen one, the false sacrificial god who required children to be sacrificed as atonement for sins; another ancient false god."

Thirteen demons materialized behind Molech and eleven poltergeists materialized behind Baal. The thirteen demons were 6 feet tall, humanoid, and appeared as dark shadowy silhouettes. The poltergeists on the other hand ranged from between 5 feet 2 inches tall and 6 feet tall with horns, long razor sharp teeth, big hands with webbed fingers and long one inch finger nails. Their appearance was similar to evil elves in Sonya's mind.

Michael glanced at Sonya as she noticed the nervousness in his eyes. Sonya as asked, "Who are they?"

Michael paused then said, "I'll explain later."

Baal said, "What you gonna do now Michael? You're outnumbered and running out of time." He giggled.

Michael said, "I'll dispatch you then be on my way."

Baal frowned, "We'll see about that."

Molech snarled, "Get him!"

The demons behind him lunged at Michael and Sonya. Michael grabbed Sonya by her collar and threw her to the ground, "Get down!" He spun swinging the rod and twirling the blades. As he swung the rod, the demons he struck dissipated while one managed to get through and clung onto his back. He punched, scratched, and bit Michael. Baal released an ear-splitting scream that echoed, "Get her!"

The eleven poltergeists behind him ran towards Sonya. Sonya ran to the door of the sporting goods store. She turned the knob and one of the poltergeists grabbed her by her sleeve and tossed her six feet across the alley. She tumbled into a wooden trash bin. Michael illuminated, jumped up and spun, striking six demons. One poltergeist bit Sonya in her side. She screamed as she pushed his face away from her. Another poltergeist kicked her repeatedly in her back. She cried, "Michael! Help me please!

Michael ran towards Sonya to help her. A poltergeist jumped onto his back. Michael flung him off. Another poltergeist clipped Michael and he stumbled. Another poltergeist grabbed him from behind and held him up. The poltergeist Michael flung off ran to him, jumped clenching onto his chest with his legs wrapped around him then punched him three times in his face bursting Michael's nose as blood sprayed. The largest poltergeist, six feet tall, yanked a two foot long one inch in diameter metal pole out of the cement and slowly walked towards Michael while another punched Michael in his stomach.

Sonya swung blindly at the poltergeists trying to defend herself. Michael took his rod and stabbed the poltergeist that held him up.

He spinned striking three poltergeists. They dissipated. Baal and Molech stood patiently watching. As Michael spinned striking demon after demon and poltergeist after poltergeist, the tallest poltergeist pierced Michael's side with the pole. Michael screamed in exquisite pain dropping his rod.

Molech said, "What a familiar sight."

Baal smirked, "Indeed it is."

The tall poltergeist jostled the pole deeper into Michael's side. Michael dropped to his knees. The tall poltergeist stood over him and said, "I've waited millenniums upon millenniums for this moment."

Michael said, "You...shouldn't have."

Michael reached down, picked up his rod, and struck the poltergeist with it. He dissipated. Michael's hand illuminated slightly as he slowly pulled the two feet long pole out of his side. The poltergeist that kicked Sonya ran towards Michael. Michael tossed the pole and picked up his rod running towards him. They both leaned their shoulder's down and collided into each other. As they collided, Michael jostled the rod through him, pulled up, and split him in half. He dissipated. Thirteen more poltergeists appeared. Michael leaned his head back and exhaled. He peered down as sweat dripped from his forehead and blood continued to drip from his nose and his side. He distressed at the sight of them; too tired not knowing if he had enough energy left to fight them and continuously bleeding as he stood in a puddle of his own blood. His eyes rolled into the back of his head and his eye lids closed as he collapsed to the ground dropping the rod with a soft clinking sound.

A poltergeist bit Sonya on her shoulder tearing her flesh as she screamed. Another hit her in her leg with a wooden stick as she howled in pain and tears sprayed from her eyes. The thirteen poltergeists slowly walked towards her growling, snarling, and slobbering. Sonya noticed Michael passed out on the ground and just knew it was over for her. She silently cried wondering what she should do as she tried to scoot away. She noticed a bright beam of light poking through the cloudy skies; odd. Jordin's voice whispered into her ears saying, "They really do have bodies of light" causing her to recall her dream. She reached up towards heaven and screamed, "Uriel!"

The clouds opened as a beam of exceedingly bright light shone through like a spot light. Uriel dropped out of the sky like a comet falling to the earth ready for battle at twelve feet tall and illuminated with a soft yellow light as his wingspan was twenty four feet across; his posture erect. His eyes sparkled like an emerald, the only portion of his face that could be seen due to his brightness. He had a seven foot long golden spear held firmly in his large hands. Thunder crashed as his feet touched the pavement and the ground rumbled. As soon as his feet touched the ground, he swung his spear striking demon after demon, poltergeist after poltergeist until none were left and none dared to appear.

Uriel stood between Molech and Baal. They walked in a counterclockwise circle around him. He stood with his head down, eyes following their every move, and circling with them. Molech snickered at Uriel while Baal snarled.

Molech shook his head in disapproval and said, "Uriel. You're not playing by the rules."

Uriel gripped the spear with both hands holding it up near his shoulder, "But I am. She called not Michael. You're not playing by the rules."

Baal said, "Aww. Isn't he cute? He thinks he's a soldier now."

Molech smirked, "Aren't you still in boot camp boy? You should know better than to think you can rock with me."

Uriel's eyebrows crumbled and his nose flared as they continued walking in circles.

Baal said, "I see The Father sent his weakest link. I was expecting a challenge someone like Gabriel maybe even Raphael. Make your move baby brother."

"After you", Uriel calmly stated as he gestured for Baal to swing first.

Molech snickered, "Leave him alone Baal. He's not a fighter. He's a nerd. Ain't you got some truth to reveal son? Go on now, go on and spread the good news and fix doctrinal errors paper pusher."

Uriel was not amused. He firmly gripped the spear, twirled it then stood into a combative stance holding the spear like someone would a baseball ball ready to swing. He stared at Molech then said, "Scared big distant brother? I see you're all talk. What? No sacrifices to fuel your ego?"

Baal stretched his hand out and a silver axe appeared. He tossed it to Molech. He stretched his hand out again and a steel mallet appeared. He held onto it firmly. Uriel stood waiting for either one of them to make a move. It was a long ten second pause. Suddenly The Adversary appeared and said, "Leave him alone. We have accomplished what we needed."

Molech frowned, "Ugh, until next time baby brother."

Uriel stated, "I look forward to it false redeemer."

Molech snarled. The Adversary said, "Enough". Molech disappeared.

Baal stared Uriel from feet to head then smirked, "Your day will come."

Uriel rebuttaled, "I look forward to hearing you scream."

Baal growled furiously in anger because he really wanted to fight Uriel. The Adversary said, "Be on." Baal disappeared.

Uriel stared into The Adversary's face like a nervous child. The Adversary smirked, "Ah! I remember the day you were created from a dying star. You remember that, do you not?"

Uriel gripped his spear, "Of course."

The Adversary glanced at the spear, "No need for that. No quarrel with you baby brother. I am only here to distract you." He smirked.

Uriel raised one eyebrow, "Distract me?"

The Adversary waved "goodbye" then said, "Go back the same way you came." He disappeared.

Uriel glanced at Michael. He went to Michael, knelt, and gently placed his hand on Michael's chest. Michael was breathing slowly and his heart was struggling to beat in his chest. Uriel knew that Michael was on the verge of bleeding to death. Uriel had the power to heal himself as all archangels did, but in order to heal Michael in the flesh, he needed assistance. On any other account, the archangels were not allowed to help Michael, but since The Adversary overstepped his bounds, this was the exception. Uriel clasped his hands together and silently called for Raphael, the archangel of healing.

Instead of dropping out of the sky, Raphael appeared kneeling next to Michael in a diffused light shaped as a transparent humanoid silhouette of nine feet tall. Uriel said, "He's almost gone."

Raphael shook his head in disapproval, "I knew he would interfere. The Father warned that he would."

"So what now?"

"We wait," Raphael said then laid hands on Michael. His hands illuminated as Michael's wounds healed. Michael opened his eyes and sprung up. He stared at Uriel, "Brother, I am so happy to see you." He turned to Raphael and hugged him, "Thank you."

"My pleasure. I must go now."

Michael shook his hand, "I understand."

Raphael vanished.

Uriel smiled at Michael, "We're watching, rooting, and waiting."

Michael searched the alley with his eyes, "Sonya. Where is she?"

"All of this was merely a distraction."

"Who has her?"

"The Adversary certainly put on quite a display."

"He must know."

"I'm sure by now he does."

"Thanks Uriel."

"Anytime; only if she calls. Until then, take care of you brother, you are quickly running out of time." Uriel spread his wings and flew away.

Michael stared at the sky watching as he vanished into thin air. Michael dropped his

head and sighed as he searched the alley with
his eyes wondering where Sonya ran off to.

CHAPTER TWENTY THREE

Jordin sat on Jensen's couch in his living room with her braced twisted ankle propped up. She wore the clothes she had on the day before. She didn't want to stay in the dorm room alone because Sonya didn't come home, and she kept hearing voices and seeing objects move on their own. The lights in her dorm room kept flicking on and off as the temperature in the room steadily dropped.

She walked to Jensen's house in the middle of the night without grabbing any of her belongings. She didn't know where else to go because her mother's house is two counties away, and she lost one of her many purses and cell phone while being chased by that girl. She couldn't call a cab without her cell phone and didn't have a penny to her name; only her mother's credit card and a bus pass. The buses stopped running at 1:00 a.m. and it was 3:00 a.m. when the chaos in the dorm began.

She sat on the couch, as the television blared in the background she decided to call her mother. She grabbed Jenson's cordless phone from the charger base on the end table next to where she sat. She dialed her mother's number. The phone rang four times before picking up, "Hello?"

"Mom. It's me." Jordin stated.

Jordin's mother, Dr. Reynolds, sat at her desk at work; a mirror image of Jordin with short hair and green eyes, she asked, "Is everything okay? You don't sound well. Why are you calling this late?"

Her eyes glistened, "Mom is there any way you can come and get me? I can't stay here anymore."

"You do this to me every year." Dr. Reynolds rubbed her forehead with the back of her hand as she shouldered the phone. "Your education is important. Ignore him baby. You are there to learn not to find a man." Dr. Reynolds opened her file drawer and pulled out a file.

"It's not about a man, mom. It's some strange things going on and I'm scared," Jordin pleaded.

"Like what?"

"I…It's…I'm being chased. Mom, this woman chased me a few weeks ago wasn't human…She crawled on the walls and made animals sounds. Her voice wasn't human. Then it happened again in the library."

Dr. Reynolds chuckled, "Come on. You've been watching too many horror films and I don't have time for this. I have enough to worry about with your sister."

Tears swelled in Jordin's eyes as she exclaimed, "Fuck her and fuck that baby. Can I get some of your time? Damn mom. I'm telling you the truth. That woman wasn't human. That woman was a demon or something. The way she growled and chased me... She was trying to kill me."

Dr. Reynolds searched through one her patient's file, "That baby is your nephew. Show some damn respect. Your sister is a high risk ten, and I don't know how many times I have to tell you this, angels, demons, spirits, none of that exists. It is a figment of your imagination. If you believe you see something supernatural then your brain will cause you to see it, when in reality, it isn't there. I think you're stressed about your breakup a few months ago and that's perfectly normal. I'll make a call to Dr. Winters to see if he can squeeze you in, not for an evaluation, just so you can speak with him about what's troubling you since I am booked well into next year, and you know I work the graveyard shift."

Jordin's eyebrows grimaced as her nose flared. She slapped her leg, "Would you stop psychologizing me for a second and just listen? I need you to be my mom right now not my Psychologist. Please just listen to me. I'm not safe here. This woman chased me down. I have a bruised hip, shoulder, and twisted ankle to prove this isn't in my head. Maybe we are wrong, mom."

Dr. Reynolds paused then closed her patient's file. She leaned back in her chair and rubbed her bottom lip, "Jordin, you are scaring me. You sound like a Schizophrenic or someone with a Delusional Disorder. I advise you to please walk into Dr. Winter's office as soon as you can. I will call him to let him know you are coming."

Tears escaped from the creases of Jordin's eyes, "I am not crazy." She wiped her tears and sniffled. "How could you believe *I* could suddenly become delusional or schizophrenic? This is me you're talking to, me." She licked her lips, shook her head, and sniffled again. "I clearly see now. People like you give things you don't understand or refuse to believe a rational, logical name to make *you* feel better. Then you turn around and teach that bullshit to us. I know mom. I know the spirit realm is real. Unexplainable? Yes. Improvable? Yes. But that doesn't make it false. I am not *fuckin'* crazy."

Dr. Reynolds paused. She took the phone away from her ear as the edges of her mouth curled and her lips pouted; quivering. The gloss of her eyes increased distorting her vision. She put the phone to her ear. "Jordin, please see Dr. Winters. I am begging you."

"Never mind mom. I don't know what I was thinking calling you of all people." She hung up the phone.

She slammed the cordless phone on the charger base. As she did that, Zoeh, stood next to the end table watching her. He stood six feet tall and was not embodied in light. Half of his face was blown off exposing particles of flesh and dried blood. Jordin couldn't see Zoeh but felt an uneasy presence. She quickly turned in the direction of the end table. She stared deeply but didn't see anything. She held back the urge to have an emotional breakdown while crumbling into her arms holding herself.

Jordin felt like a wounded animal in a sea of sharks not understanding how she got there. She was being preyed upon by beings she could not see, did not know, and did not understand. Was she driving herself crazy? Was she truly insane? Was the spirit realm real? If so, why was it obscure; unnoticed?

As she was deep in thought fighting to hold back her tears, Jensen came to her with a cup of cocoa in his hands. He handed it to her and said, "Are you okay?"

Jordin took the cocoa, "Thank you. I'll be fine. Just spoke with the woman I call mother." She took a sip of the cocoa.

Jensen walked to the love seat and sat down, "Must have been an argument, hunh? Do you want to talk about it?"

Jordin took a sip of the cocoa, "Are you open minded?"

"Yes. I was a Wiccan remember?"

"Do you believe in the spirit realm?" Jordin leaned up to place the coffee onto the coffee table.

Jensen put his arm on the armrest, "Of course I do. I'd be a fool not to."

Jordin paused for a few seconds staring at the black wrought iron, glass topped coffee table. She bit the tip of her fingernail, "What if I told you I'm being haunted by a demon? What if I told you I was chased by a demon possessed woman and that is how I twisted my ankle? Would you think I'm crazy?"

Jensen stated, "No. I wouldn't because I believe you."

"Why? I don't even believe myself although I know she wasn't human. Why can't I fathom it?" She shook her head and smacked her lips.

Jensen leaned up, placing his elbows on his knees, "I think you do fathom it and you believe it. I think you're afraid of what people will think once they find out you finally believe it. Since I've known you, you've played by your own rules. You never conformed. Being different and out there was you. That was your thing. I think being like everybody else scares you."

"How does a quiet kid know so much?" Jordin smiled intrigued by Jensen's wisdom.

"Because we watch people while others interact with people. You'd be surprised what you can find out by sitting on the sidelines. FYI it is okay to believe in something greater than yourself. It's not a sign of weakness. It's a sign of hope and a desire to be something greater." Jensen rubbed the peach fuzz on his chin.

"Never thought of it like that. I'm confused inside, you know? Not knowing scares me." Jordin stared at the royal blue carpeted floor.

"Some things in life are not meant for us to understand or to know. As a matter of fact, stay right here and don't follow me." Jensen got up and went down the hall. At the end of the hall, was a door with three dead bolt locks on it. He unlocked the door and walked down the stairs into the basement of the two bedroom one story house. Jordin sat on the couch in a state of bewilderment.

After about five minutes, Jensen returned with a beautiful antiqued pewter ring. The design of the ring was an inscription in an ancient Sumerian language; it was absolutely beautiful and had a total of thirteen gemstones on it, one large oval black onyx encircled by the birthstones and signs of the zodiac.

Jensen grabbed Jordin's leg, moved the pillow that propped it, sat down, and placed her legs across his lap. She stared at him wondering what he was doing. Jensen grabbed Jordin's right hand, spread her fingers, as she stared into his eyes. She realized how beautiful his eyes truly were as he slid the ring onto her middle finger and said, "Wow. It's a perfect fit…As long as you wear this ring, you will be protected. You won't have to be afraid of anything. Do you believe that?"

Jordin stared at the ring as she leaned towards Jensen smiling with a slight blush, "Thank you. I'm not sure I do but you seem to be the only one so far who believes me other than Sonya and Adriana. Actually, the only person I told how I really feel. It's nice to know you don't think I'm crazy or delusional. Thank you for everything… and I'm sorry."

"Sorry for what?"

"How I played you. You know…had a one night stand with you then bounced."

"No Problem. I'm not worried about that. It is what it is, but you can stay here as long as you like. I'll always be here for you."

Jordin ran her fingers through her hair, "Do you believe in God?"

Jensen smirked, "No. God is nothing more than a philosophy. We are god."

"How are we God?"

"God is in us. Everything in the universe is interrelated and interdependent. All of the elements in the atmosphere of the universe, in the soil of the earth, can be found within our own bodies. The universe is God and God is the universe."

"How can you believe in demons but not believe in God?"

"I don't believe in demons, but I know what you meant by calling them demons. There are higher beings in this world in the spiritual realm. Some have evolved and reached the higher state of consciousness that we all have the potential to reach. Others serve as teachers to mankind…I've seen them."

Jordin sat up and removed her leg from across Jensen's lap, "What do they look like?"

"Like you and I. Some are smaller than us and others are bigger than us."

"So you talk to evil spirits?"

"No. I talk to enlightened ones."

"You're creeping me out." She stood.

"Where are you going?"

"Back to my dorm…but thanks for everything though."

Jensen stood, "Look, I'm not trying to scare you. If you could just hear what they have to say, you'll understand. There's nothing to be afraid of."

"The only thing I wanna understand is why me? Everything else is meaningless as of right now. No offense, but should have known better than to trust an ex-wiccan."

Jensen giggled sarcastically, "Well, be on then."

Jordin raised her left eyebrow, "Far as I know, you could have something to do with this. Stay away from me Jensen."

"No problem."

Jordin left slamming the door behind her. Beliah appeared to Jensen and said, "The Adversary is going to kill you."

Jensen said, "Not before he kills you. I still have time to make this right with him. You don't, so instead of worrying about me, you need to hide."

Beliah smirked and sighed, "You can't make it right with him, ever. There are no second chances with him. Once he finds out, I don't even want to see it; gruesome it will be."

Jensen frowned, "Find out what?"

CHAPTER TWENTY FOUR

Darkness filled the dorm room with the exception of the light from the moon gleaming between the opened white blinds and the light from the hallway spilling under the door. Adriana was nestled in her bed lying on her side in a fetal position holding herself tight as she lain across the top of her comforter. Her forehead glistened in response to the heat of the room as her medium length dark brown hair was wrapped under a multi-colored scarf. Muffled sounds of students talking in the hallway was the only sound that could be heard but not by the sleeping Adriana.

She turned to the other side as her bed creaked with her body's rotation. "Wake up", a voice whispered. Adriana still asleep did not hear it. She wiped the sweat from her forehead with the back of her hand then wiped her hand on her tank top as she slept. "Kill Jordin", the voice whispered louder. Adriana turned her head digging in her ear while still asleep. The voice muttered, "Its Jordin. The mother of the abomination. Kill her." Adriana quickly opened her eyes because she heard that. Her eyes wide open as she pierced through the dark room. She said, "Leave me alone." She heard a voice giggle like that of a small child. Adriana sat up in her bed clenching one of her pillows. The voice said, "The mother of the abomination. Kill Jordin before it's too late." Adriana quickly reached over to her night stand and clicked the light on. She said, "Leave me alone. Just leave me alone." The voice giggled as it echoed a bit; the sound of a small child. Adriana sat frozen for a spell piercing the dorm room with her eyes. The voice didn't say anything else.

Adriana climbed out of bed and walked barefoot to the other side of the dorm room. She clicked the light in that lamp on. She walked to the dorm room door, locked it then clicked the light switch turning on the overhead light. She returned to her bed and sat on the edge of it. She opened the top drawer of her night stand and pulled out a small four ounce glass and a medium sized bottle of Vodka. Not really a drinker, Adriana poured herself a shot and inhaled it all.

Adriana poured two more shots and quickly ingested them. She sat the bottle and the glass on the night stand next to her bible and in front of the small desk lamp. She sat in her bed with her knees folded up to her chest. She grabbed three of her four pillows placing them between her back and the wall, because her bed didn't have a headboard, and sat propped up. She was one of the few students in a double room without a roommate. Her dorm room was warmer than normal because she left with the heat on 80 degrees earlier that day, so she sat on top of her beige comforter terrified.

With no shoes or socks on her feet, she changed positions and sat with her legs crossed as her gym shorts rode up her behind. A faint knock on the door interrupted the silence of the room starling her a bit. Adriana slid out of bed and crept to the door on her tip toes because she hated walking barefoot on tile floors. She said, "Who is it?" Jordin replied, "It's me. Open up."

Adriana paused. She remembered Ayana's warning to stay away from Jordin and Sonya, at the same time she was terrified to stay in that dorm by herself and really needed some sleep. Jordin said, "Hello? You gonna let me in or what?" Adriana unlocked the top lock and opened the door. Jordin stood there with her hair pulled into a raggedy pony tail with bags under her eyes. Adriana said, "Sleepless night?"

Jordin walked in and said, "You have no idea. I see you must be having one too. These lights are bright. What are these? 100 watt bulbs?"

Adriana quickly tip toed back to her bed, "No, I think 75 watts. Unsure."

Jordin shut and locked the dorm room door. She tossed her coat into the chair by the door, kicked her sneakers off then climbed onto the empty bed. She lain across it stomach down, stretched, and said, "Damn chick. You got it on hell in here."

"Yeah, I know complete accident. Comfty?"

"Yes, I'm so damn tired. I think I'm failing all of my classes."

"You're not the only one. I haven't been to class in two weeks. What brings you out at after 4 in the morning?"

"Sonya didn't come home and some strange shit was going on. I can't stay there no more. I'm thinking about packing my shit and going home."

"You're not the only one. Sonya didn't come home? That's unlike her. I wonder if she's okay."

"I don't know, and right now, I don't care. I just know I can't be alone in that room and I need to get away from her. She's ruining my life. Her and that whack job Jensen."

"Jensen?"

"Yeah, went to his place just to find out he talks to demons and shit. Is there any place safe on this fucking earth? I really need to find Michael."

"Who?"

"That man that was watching me. He's my protector. I should have gotten an address. Stupid me," Jordin glanced over at the night stand next to Adriana and noticed the bottle of Vodka and the empty glass, "What are you of all people doing drinking?"

"These damn voices driving me to drink," She smirked.

Jordin smirked as she glanced at the glass, "You got another one of them?"

Adriana peered over at her glass, "A glass?"

"Nope. I was talking about something else."

Adriana smirked, "This is the only glass I have but you're welcome to have some if you need it." Adriana leaned over to her night stand and grabbed the glass. She leaned over and handed it to Jordin, "Be careful. That'll put hair on your chest."

Jordin grabbed the glass, "Fuck hair on my chest. I'm looking to grow a damn beard, you heard me?"

Adriana giggled, "I hear you."

Jordin downed the glass, rubbed her chest, frowned then handed the glass back to Adriana. Adriana smirked, "Another round?"

"Hell yeah."

Adriana filled the four ounce glass with vodka then handed it to Jordin. Instead of inhaling it, she lightly sipped the glass. Jordin said, "So this is how you've been coping?"

"Yep, when things happen, I wake up, turn the lights on, and get as drunk as I can. Alcohol seems to drown out the voices, and they never come out and show themselves with the lights on."

"How do you know that?" Jordin took a sip of her drink.

"Experience…and Ayana."

"Ayana? You mean the woman you call the evil hoo-doo queen?"

"Yes, and I was wrong about her. I can admit that. She told me our problem is mainly because of Sonya. The evil spirits are attached to her due to a near death experience she had when she was 6 years old. You know anything about that?"

Jordin took a sip of her drink, "Sure do. I was there. We were riding with Mrs. Nathan; it was cold and rainy outside. We slid on the road and hit a tree. Sonya's seatbelt snapped and she went through the windshield. Recovery took over a year and she had to have open spine surgery and some other types of surgeries. She was just so small. I was lucky though. I barely had a scratch on me…but that doesn't make any sense. I was chased first. I saw them first." Jordin took a sip of her drink.

"Doesn't mean anything. Ayana said she brought a spirit back with her when she died for three minutes. The same spirit terrorizing you. It's probably the same one that speaks to me."

"Still doesn't make sense. Sonya wasn't there tonight and tonight was much worse than previous nights. My bed actually shook like we were having an earthquake or something and something kept growling from under my bed."

Adriana took a swig of the large bottle of vodka, "Have you checked under your bed?"

Jordin took a sip of her glass, "Hell nah, I got the fuck up out of there."

"Well, I was reading a book about a woman that was a doorway for evil spirits. Trust me, check under your bed. If something's there, I'll explain why."

Jordin stared at the bottle of Vodka then smirked, "This is too funny. The saint getting drunk?"

"Nah, not a joking matter at all, and I'm far from a saint."

"Why don't you just pray about it?" Jordin snickered.

Adriana threw a pillow at her smirking, "So not funny."

The voice whispered to Adriana, "Kill Jordin." Adriana covered her ears with her hands and silently said, "Just leave me alone." The voice giggled. Jordin could not hear the voice at all. She noticed Adriana covering her ears and said, "You hear something?"

"I'm tripping. How about we go check under your bed?"

CHAPTER TWENTY FIVE

Jensen crept through the back yard of Mr. and Mrs. Nathan, Sonya's parents, wearing a black pair of jeans, a thick black waist length coat, black leather gloves, a pair of black combat boots, with an empty black duffle bag within his grasp. He leaned up against the tree that resided in the middle of their back yard near the four feet tall twelve feet diameter above ground swimming pool. He peaked around and stared into the window from the distance. The kitchen light was on with the curtains wide open. No one was seen moving around. Jensen glanced at the black sports watch on his left wrist. It read 4:45 a.m. He rubbed his hands together and blew into them and he shivered. The thin leather gloves did nothing to keep the cold from penetrating his fingertips. It was five degrees this dark silent morning. He wished he could wait another day, preferably a warmer day because it was unseasonably cold, but he was a few hours shy of running out of time. He had a very small window to kill Mr. Nathan and take the trumpets as well luring Michael to The Adversary.

As the crescent moon light illuminated the sky, Jensen peered up. The crescent moon with a star in its center was the symbol of witchcraft. The symbolism was positive for him yet his nerves still got the best of him. Although he knew the Nathan's were asleep, he had never pulled off a home invasion. It was much easier for him to capture his victims by surprise while out instead of like this. He had murdered over twenty five people at The Adversary's command, some for sacrifices and others because they were simply in the way. Jensen had never been caught for his crimes and had a bad feeling in his gut that this might be that one time too many.

Jensen took in a deep breath then exhaled slowly. He opened his coat and pulled out a 9 mm handgun from the inside pocket. He made sure the magazine was fully loaded. He put the duffle bag straps over his shoulders to carry it like a back pack then he crept up the side of the yard along the safety of the darkness that bordered the fence. As he crept up towards the house alongside of the fence, Beliah appeared to him. Jensen stopped with an expression of irritation on his face, "This is not the fucking time." Beliah stood in front of him with his arms crossed in disapproval, "I've warned you. This is my last warning."

"I don't have a choice, okay. I do this and get the damn trumpets then we'll be on good terms again."

"You are so foolish", Beliah stated as he shook his head in disapproval while smirking. He continued, "Carry on." Beliah disappeared.

Jensen frowned. He shook his head in disapproval as he continued towards the back patio. He slowly crept up the five stairs of the oak wood deck holding the gun firmly within his grasp. He walked past the patio set peeking into the kitchen window. No one was in sight. He pulled a key out of his pants pocket. It was Sonya's house key. He unlocked the door and slightly pushed it open waiting to hear an alarm go off. There was nothing except the sound of the heat coming up from the furnace. Jensen smirked. He said to himself, *this is going to be easier than I thought.* He opened the door and went in slowly while quietly pulling the door closed behind him.

Inside of the kitchen, Jensen quickly crept into the living room from beside the refrigerator that rested next to the back door to be within the darkness and not so exposed. In the living room, he searched around with his eyes while he held the gun with both of his hands. As Jensen slowly crept through the living room on his way towards the dining room, Mr. Nathan sat in his den watching him on the surveillance camera.

Mr. Nathan, a short 5 feet 6 inch tall stocky built man, sat with his hand against his face. His dark green eyes unafraid yet his eyebrows revealed a hint of concern. He glanced at a sterling silver chest containing four locks that rested next to his desk. He sent a text to his wife who was sleeping upstairs in their bed. Mr. Nathan stood then walked towards the door of the den.

Jensen crept into the dining room looking around at the decorative items. He noticed a picture of Sonya when she was about seven years old on the curio cabinet. She was wearing two long pigtails, hugging a golden retriever puppy, and smiling with her two front teeth missing. He heard a sound as he diverted his attention to the door of the den. He didn't see a light under the door, but the door had an engraved sign that read "Nathan Contracting". Jensen stopped and thought to himself, *nah that would be too obvious.* Jensen had the urge to go in to see what he could find, but thought otherwise. He figured the trumpets would not actually be in the house. They'd be in a safe location maybe even hidden under ground. His plan was to murder the wife and kidnap Mr. Nathan, have him show him where the trumpets were then murder him too.

Jensen saw the staircase next to the den. He turned away from the den proceeding towards the stairs. As soon as Jensen stepped on the first step, it creaked loudly. Jensen quickly removed his foot leaning up against the wall to remain out of sight in case one of the Nathan's heard the creak of the stairs. He poked his head around the corner and looked up the stairs. Not one light turned on nor did he hear anything. He smirked. "What is it you want?" Mr. Nathan said. Jensen gripped the gun so tight if his gloves were not on his hands his fingertips would be white. Jensen heard him speak but could not see him. Jensen turned his head in the direction of the voice. Jensen didn't say one word because he did not want Mr. Nathan to know his location. Jensen was afraid to move.

A bullet punctured the wall three inches above his head as plaster from the wall sprinkled down. Jensen ran alongside of the wall the door of the den posted leaning against the corner. He felt trapped, "Hey man, no need for all of that. I just wanted to steal a few things. I need my fix."

"Get out of my house", Mr. Nathan said.

Jensen clearly heard him and from the sound of his voice knew his location. Jensen fired three shots at Mr. Nathan who knelt in the dining room near the table behind a chair. Jensen said, "I'm not trying to hurt you dude. Put the gun down and we can talk about this."

Mr. Nathan chuckled.

Jensen said, "I'm not playing man. I'll light this motherfucker up. I'm trying to be peaceable. You piss me off and everybody dies."

Mr. Nathan chuckled again. He clapped and the light above the door of the den turned on so bright it was almost blinding. Jensen trembled firing his gun as he tried to run towards the other part of the living room where the lights were off. As he ran, Mr. Nathan shot him three times. Jensen dropped to the floor still alive but badly wounded; three shots to the trunk of his chubby body. Mr. Nathan calmly walked towards him with his hand gun drawn. Jensen laid on his side holding himself shaking as he coughed blood and a rattling sound was heard coming from his lungs. Mrs. Nathan stood at the top of the stairs in her bathrobe. Mr. Nathan said, "Call this thief an ambulance." As she walked off, she said, "Sure."

As Jensen lay bleeding to death, Beliah appeared. Jensen's eyes got as big as quarters. He said, "You?" Beliah smirked. Mr. Nathan turned to Beliah and said, "Thank you." Beliah said, "No problem", he stared at Jensen and said, "Now who's going to be screaming?" Jensen took his last breath as the sounds of the ambulance became audible. Beliah disappeared.

CHAPTER TWENTY SIX

Jordin and Adriana walked into Jordin and Sonya's dorm. Jordin clicked on the light switch that posted on the wall adjacent to the door. She tossed her purse onto the metal chair that rested in the corner under the coat rack. Her purse slid across the seat onto the floor. She nervously stared at Adriana and took in a deep breath exhaling slowly. Adriana appeared a little frightened as well. Jordin said, "Here we go."

They slowly crept towards the bed as the temperature in the room steadily began to drop. Jordin knocked all of the pillows off of the bed onto the cold tile floor. Adriana, only wearing a pair of cotton slip on shoes without strings or laces, felt cold air coming from underneath the bed. She said, "Jordin, do you feel that?" Jordin appeared puzzled, "Feel what?"

Adriana looked down and noticed Jordin was wearing light brown Eskimo styled boots with the fur hanging out of them. She said, "That cold you feel when you're in here by yourself is coming from underneath your bed."

Jordin walked to the left side of the end of the bed, "Grab that end."

Adriana grabbed the right end of the bed. Jordin said, "On three. 1…2…3."

They both lifted up the bed. Adriana's eyes bulged as Jordin's mouth opened wide. There was a large pentagram drawn underneath the bed in a thick chalk like substance with the numbers 666 drawn into a triangle in the middle. Cold fog was flowing from the center like when someone speaks outside in the winter time. It was thin and slightly transparent. The temperature of the room dropped considerably. Jordin said, "What the fuck?"

"Ayana was wrong. Sonya's not the doorway. This is the doorway."

"What the fuck are you talking about? Who put this shit under my bed?"

"According to the book I read, high priests of witchcraft typically mark people by putting these doorways underneath their beds so spirits can come and go at will."

They both looked at each other and said at the same time, "Jensen."

Jordin paused then said, "But why would he do that?"

"You've been chosen." A voice they could not see muttered as they saw a hand. The hand had six fingers with long sharp pointy finger nails coming up from the center of the encircled pentagram. The floor appeared gaseous and foggy. They both screamed dropping the bed and ran towards the door. As they ran towards the door screaming frantically, Mrs. Reynolds and two Sheriff's, one female and the other male, walked in.

Jordin ran directly into her mother almost knocking her down still screaming with Adriana close upon her heels. Mrs. Reynolds said, "What is going on?"

Jordin quickly blurted, "There's something coming out from under my bed!"

Mrs. Reynolds slapped Jordin and said, "Calm down. Now what is going on with all this screaming?"

"I promise momma. Something tried to climb up out of the floor from underneath my bed."

Adriana agreed, "Mom, she's not lying. I saw it too."

Mrs. Reynolds smacked her lips together in irritation. She stared at Adriana and Jordin for a few seconds then said, "You're drunk. The both of you." She crossed her arms then continued, "Why is it so cold in here?"

Jordin put her hands on her head distressfully, "Mom the Vodka has nothing to do with it. It was just a few shots."

Adriana said, "Mom, just check under the bed and see for yourself."

Mrs. Reynolds glanced at the two Sheriff's deputy's smirking. They both snickered as they shook their heads in disapproval. Mrs. Reynolds said, "I've seen and heard enough. Cuff her."

The two Sheriff's deputy's grabbed Jordin. She pulled away from them resisting, "Mom, what are you doing? What did I do?"

"I know you don't understand this now but you will thank me later."

Jordin paused staring as her mother puzzled, "For fucking real? You're committing me? The fuck is wrong with you?"

"It's for your own benefit baby. Momma is going to get you the help you need."

Adriana said, "You're committing her? She did nothing wrong. She's not crazy."

Mrs. Reynolds pointed her finger down into Adriana's face. At six feet tall she stood a good 5 1/5 inches taller than her. She said, "Watch it girly or you're next with your drunk ass. Talking about ghosts, demons, and shit. Chemically induced hallucinations that's what they are. What else are y'all on?"

Adriana frowned, "Excuse me? I don't fucking use drugs, and if you knew half of what we've been through these past few weeks, you'd fucking understand. And to think, I once had a lot of respect for you. Not so much so right now. You're truly a bitch."

"In all caps with 1,000 exclamation points behind it!"

The female sheriff approached Jordin. As soon as she got within two feet of her, Jordin punched her in her face. The female sheriff stumbled back as her nose bled. The male sheriff grabbed Jordin's shoulder as she moved away from him. She threw objects from her dresser at them; perfume bottles, deodorant, hair brushes, etc as they tried to dodge the items. The female sheriff drew her gun and pointed it at Jordin, "Stop it, stop it now." The male sheriff put his hands out in front of him with his fingers spread and said, "Come on now. Just come peacefully. We don't want this to get ugly now do we?"

Mrs. Reynolds said, "Jordin, stop it this instant. She will shoot you. Now come on."

Adriana rolled her eyes in disbelief and crossed her arms. Tears fell from Jordin's eyes, "How could you do this to me? I'm not stupid mom. You told them I'm a danger to myself and others. I'm not a danger to anyone and you know that. How could you lie like that? I'm your own fucking child. How could you believe after all of these years that I could turn crazy over night? Science and your disbelief in anything intangible have truly fucked up your ability to reason."

Mrs. Reynolds' eyes glossed but she held on to her stern demeanor, "This is for your own good."

Tears escaped from the creases of Adriana's eyes, "Don't worry Jordin. I'll figure something out."

"You can't help her."

"I promise I will do everything in my power to make you lose your PhD. Don't *ever* slip up. You better *always* dot your "I's" and cross your "T's"."

"I don't take threats from ex-strippers. Bet that's something you didn't know about your little friend Jordin. She has *lots* of little secrets."

Adriana's eyebrows crumbled as she emotionlessly said, "Watch yourself." She walked out of the dorm room.

Jordin dropped her head as the male sheriff placed hand cuffs around her wrists.

CHAPTER TWENTY SEVEN

Michael exited Sonya and Jordin's residence hall with a distressed expression on his face. He had gone back and forth from their dorm to the abandoned building he stayed in search of Sonya fearing the worse but was hopeful that she was simply so frightened that she ran away. He could only imagine the thoughts that went through her head during the attack. As a human being, she had never witnessed anything like that before, and the flash of the terrified expression on her face when she screamed for him to help her, haunted him. He felt a deep sense of shame which was an emotion so very foreign to him for not being able to protect her. He knew that he was now completely human and his time was extremely short. The clock was ticking against Michael and ear piercingly clear.

The early morning was frigid as a few snowflakes trickled down from the skies above. Michael did not have on a coat just an old sweater with a brown t-shirt underneath. His coat was ripped during the fight in the alley, and without careful thought, he walked away without it. He hugged himself as he walked briskly against the flow of the wind. The silver rod in his back pocket sticking up his back underneath his sweater didn't help either. With every step, the cold rod touched his back with the cold penetrating the t-shirt. His hands were so cold that he placed them underneath his underarms as his body shuddered and his teeth chattered.

As Michael approached the park to use it as a short cut to get back to the building, Beliah appeared to him. Normally Michael would stop to see what he wanted, but it was much too cold for that this morning. Michael glanced at Beliah continuing on his way. Beliah followed alongside of him. Michael said, "What now?"

"I know where Sonya is."

Michael stopped in his tracks staring at him. Beliah grinned, "I see that got your attention."

Michael frowned then continued walking. Beliah caught up to him and said, "Seriously, all tricks and games aside. I know exactly where she is."

"Then tell me where she is."

"Not so fast brother. Information isn't free anymore. You give me what I want and I'll make sure you get what you want. Good old earthly bargaining."

Michael's left eyebrow raised as he glanced at Beliah, "I'm listening."

"I want a meeting with The Father."

Michael giggled, "You can't be serious."

"Oh, but I am."

Michael paused. He stopped and stared at Beliah. He diverted his attention to the ground then glanced back up at him, "You're truly on your own accord?"

"Been trying to get you to see that since the diner."

"Who's Darkness and why does he want her?"

"I don't know who she is. I was hoping you could tell me, but what I do know is why he *needs* her."

"Well, enlighten me."

"He calls her darkness because that is the essence of her character; selfish, manipulative, adulterous, promiscuous etcetera, etcetera. She's a sociopath incapable of loving anyone or anything other than herself. Similar to him, she deceives and manipulates everyone she comes into contact with and hides well behind good deeds, a smile, fake emotions, personality, and her religion."

Michael bit the bottom of his chapped lip then said, "Okay, she's as evil as he. What does that have to do with anything? What does that have to do with Sonya?"

"Darkness is the woman he has chosen to carry his seed, and she is a close friend of Sonya."

"Jordin?" Michael appeared stunned then continued, "So, he's trying to get Sonya out of the way so he can have Jordin?"

"No, Sonya's dreams are how he knows your purpose. You know? The trumpets."

"Does he have them?"

"Not yet, but you better act *really* fast."

"What do you want with The Father?"

"I just need a message delivered. I want a meeting."

Michael cut him off, "You have been down here a little too long. Have you forgotten? I am not a messenger of The Father, Gabriel is. You want to deliver a message then you have to send it through him."

"You're the closest to The Father."

"Your meeting sounds urgent, and I don't have the time. I have a mission of my own and I'm running out of time."

"I know you're limited. Call him."

"I will."

"Well, what are you waiting for?"

Michael placed his hands together, bowed his head, and closed his eyes. He whispered, "Father, please summon Gabriel." He opened his eyes, lifted his head, and hugged himself again to shield against the cold.

Gabriel flew down from the sky at close to the speed of light. He landed gracefully onto the frozen grass. He stood nine feet tall, wearing a white silk robe, humanoid with red hair and light blue eyes. He was lean yet strong and appeared older and wiser than the other arch angels, "You called."

Michael pointed at Beliah. Gabriel glanced at him. Beliah said, "I would like for you to deliver a message to The Father."

Gabriel said, "Go on."

"I have spent millenniums upon millenniums on this earth in the deepest resentment. I have turned millions of people towards The Father to save them from the manipulation and deception that caused me to fall many aeons ago. I desire a meeting with him. Although my fate is sealed without any chance of redemption, I would like the honor of throwing the false prophets of the earth into the abyss."

Gabriel's eyebrows crumbled in disbelief, "Hmmm, is that all?"

"That is all."

"I will deliver it now." Gabriel flew away.

Michael stared at Beliah, "Where is she?"

CHAPTER TWENTY EIGHT

Pastor Jones pulled up in front of Mr. Nathan's house in his black flatbed pick-up truck. The early morning hours annoyed him because it reminded him of his lost position in the heavens. He remembered playing beautiful music at dawn as the angels delighted. He had been placed on a pedestal by all in the heavens. He was not only the most beautiful angel he was also the strongest. Although he did not want to admit nor face it, he missed playing music in the heavens. He stared at the bible in his passenger seat. He remembered the verse written about him that stated: "You were the model of perfection, full of wisdom and perfect in beauty." He said to himself, *as I remain; perhaps even wiser and more beautiful now.*

Pastor Jones grabbed the bible from the passenger seat and sat it in his lap. He grabbed his dark gray trench coat from behind him and slid it on. He turned the truck off mumbling to himself, *Must I do everything myself.* He grimaced shaking his head in disapproval, grabbed the bible then got out of the truck.

This morning was bitterly cold, and for the first time, The Adversary felt the temperature in his new flesh. He shivered as he briskly walked across the street with the bible held firmly within his grasp. As he walked, a car sped down the street towards him. He immobilized the car with a stare as he continued to walk as though the car was frozen in time. The driver of the vehicle said, "What the fuck?" as he stared at Pastor Jones. As soon as he touched the sidewalk, the car continued on down the street. The male driver of the vehicle slammed on the brakes almost wrecking into a parked car as he stared at him in disbelief.

Pastor Jones stepped onto the wooden porch and knocked firmly on the door. He adjusted his silver neck tie making sure it was perfect around his neck. Mr. Nathan cracked the door peering out, "May I help you?"

Pastor Jones gave a beautiful, friendly smile, "Yes, my name is Pastor William Jones from Jones' Temple."

"Okay."

"I know your daughter Sonya. I don't know if you heard but Pastor Mason Ryan was murdered not too long ago."

Mr. Nathan placed his hand over his mouth in disbelief. Pastor Ryan was the family's minister. Mr. Nathan grew up knowing him although he no longer attended church. Pastor Ryan married him and his wife. "Wow…Who would do something like that?"

"Evil…absolutely evil. May I come in and speak with you for a bit? It's about Sonya."

"Sonya? What's wrong with her?"

"She has taken his death rather hard, and I'd like to speak with you about her and offer suggestions on how *we* can help with her grief."

While opening the door to allow Pastor Jones to enter, "Sure, come on in. We can speak in my den."

Pastor Jones entered the house following Mr. Nathan to his den. On the walk through he said, "You have a lovely home."

Mr. Nathan replied, "Thank you."

"Sonya told me she and her mother are very close."

"They are."

"Is the misses' home? Maybe we should include her in this discussion."

"Oh, she's at work. Won't be home until 5 this afternoon."

Mr. Nathan unlocked the door of the den and let himself in. Pastor Jones followed him inside. Mr. Nathan motioned for him to sit across from him on the other side of his desk. Pastor Jones sat while looking around the den. He immediately eyed the locked silver trunk. Mr. Nathan said, "So what's going on with my baby girl?"

"Where do I begin? She's been having terrible nightmares about Lucifer. She believes he is trying to tell her something. She hasn't been sleeping well and spends her days alone crying and drinking heavily. She hasn't been to class."

"Hmmm…that doesn't sound like my Sonya. When her grandmother, my wife's mother, passed, she didn't shed one tear."

"Well, things have changed since then. It's not every day you find out your best friend is sleeping with your boyfriend then the very next day your Pastor whom you love like a grandfather is found dead. That's enough to make even the strongest person snap."

Mr. Nathan rubbed his hands together as he leaned up to put his elbows onto the desk, "I suppose. Yeah, Jordin is a mess, but we can't pick our kids friends for them. She is certainly her mother's child. So what can we do? She's not going to stop being friends with Jordin, and I know this must be killing her inside. Maybe I should call her?"

"Not a good idea. That is why I am here. Sonya has been missing for the past three days. No one knows where she is and we thought maybe you could give us an idea where she could have gone."

Mr. Nathan scratched his head, "The only place I can think of is moms, but mom is in the hospital. Has anyone checked Greene Memorial?"

"Yes, we did. Jordin gave us the same suggestion…May I ask what is that?" Pastor Jones pointed to the locked silver trunk.

"Oh it's just a trunk that's been in my family for about a hundred years. Given to us by cousins of my ancestors."

"Whatever's in it must be precious for it to contain so many locks. It's beautiful. I've never seen anything like it before. May I?"

"Sure."

Pastor Jones walked towards the trunk. He knelt beside it and gently rubbed the rounded inscribed corners with the tips of his fingers. The language was ancient Hebrew. He said, "This must be worth millions. Is this pure sterling silver?"

"Yes, and no it's not worth millions", Mr. Nathan chuckled then continued, "about a few hundred thousand though."

"Splendid it is. What's in it?"

"Just an antique that has been in my family for ages."

Pastor Jones smirked, "Trumpets?"

Mr. Nathan appeared shocked, "What do you mean?"

Pastor Jones stood with a blank expression on his face, "I'm going to take the trumpets with me if you don't mind."

Mr. Nathan pulled out a hand gun and pointed it at Pastor Jones, "The hell you will? Get out now or I will shoot."

Pastor Jones smirked. He blinked and the two windows in the den on the adjacent wall to the desk burst open towards the inside. Mr. Nathan dropped the gun covering his head to shield himself from the flying glass, but his arms were cut anyway. Mr. Nathan said, "Oh God."

"Your God isn't here right now."

Mr. Nathan picked up the gun. With a stare from Pastor Jones, the gun flew out of Mr. Nathan's hand outside of the window. Mr. Nathan glanced at the opened door of the den then attempted to run towards it. Pastor Jones ran behind him wrapping his arms around his arms releasing an earsplitting lion's roar and drooling. Mr. Nathan screamed and started to pray aloud, but Pastor Jones tossed him across the room. He hit the wall near the locked silver trunk sliding to the floor. Pastor Jones said, "Unlock it."

"No. You can't have it."

"Foolish soul. You're willing to die for this. You're going to hell anyway. Why should you care? Now open it."

"I said no."

"Very well then. You will die."

Pastor Jones calmly strode towards Mr. Nathan. Mr. Nathan stood in a combative stance. As soon as Pastor Jones got within his intimate space, Mr. Nathan punched him in his nose. Pastor Jones' nose broke as blood sprayed, but he did not flinch. He quickly reached his hand out and penetrated Mr. Nathan's chest. Pastor Jones hand firmly gripped his heart. Mr. Nathan moaned in excruciating pain as his knees faltered. Pastor Jones ripped Mr. Nathan's heart out of his body as it still beat in his hand. He tossed it to the floor as Mr. Nathan's body dropped.

Pastor Jones knelt by the locked silver trunk. He ripped each and every lock off then opened the four feet long by two feet high by one feet depth metal trunk. He sighed then screamed in fury kicking Mr. Nathan's body as hard as he could, "Fuck! Motherfuck!" He stomped his head until his skull was completely crushed leaving Mr. Nathan's face unrecognizable. He rubbed the blood from the bottom of his alligator-skinned dress shoes by rubbing his feet into the carpet. He sighed as he ran his fingers through his long hair to collect himself. He bent down and lifted the long silver keyless trumpet out of the trunk. He said to himself aloud, "Where's the other?"

.

CHAPTER TWENTY NINE

Michael turned around and headed towards the campus. He needed to pass through the campus to get to Sonya's location. He was freezing to the point of shivering as he hoped Belie told him the truth of her whereabouts. He tried to analyze and rationalize all that Belie had told him. It made sense but at the same time didn't. He wondered if it was possible for The Father and The Adversary to have chosen the same woman. Was it possible that Sonya was chosen to help him because of her lineage but was also chosen by The Adversary due to her lineage? What better a disguise could the man of perdition have than to have Hebrew blood even if it was only a remnant?

Michael sneezed as he approached the campus library. His eyes lit up as he hastened his pace. He knew he could sit in the library for a while to get warm. As some students were walking out, he caught the door and walked inside. He rubbed his hands together in an attempt to warm his fingertips. The tips of his fingers tingled painfully as they began to thaw. He wandered around the library in search of a secluded place to sit where he would go unnoticed until he warmed up. As he approached the fiction section, he saw Adriana and Ayana sitting across from each other at a table for six, with three wooden chairs on each side, leaning towards each other talking. The two of them talking was not what caught and held his attention. What caught and held his attention was seeing Belie slide inside of Ayana. Michael leaned against the book shelf just watching them.

Adriana said, "I don't understand."

Belie spoke through Ayana, "You of all people should."

"This is just too much for me right now. This is too much," Adriana distressingly said as she ran her fingers through her hair.

"I say you leave town immediately. Go to a secluded location where no one can find you. This is the only way you'll be safe. They have your friends. It's only a matter of time before they have you too."

Michael walked over to them. He stared at Ayana and said, "May I have a word with you?"

Ayana smirked, "This is Jordin's Michael. Michael this is Adriana."

Michael nodded his head, "Nice to meet you, but I need a word with you."

Ayana stood, "I'll be right back."

She followed Michael towards the card catalog. Michael said, "What are you doing?"

"I'm helping."

"How so?"

"By keeping her safe. Pastor Jones isn't Pastor Jones. The Adversary inhabits him.

Jordin has been committed by her mother, and Sonya has been moved."

"What do you mean she's been moved?"

"You just don't get it Michael. He's not going to let you win again. The longer you remain in your flesh the weaker you become. The longer he remains in his flesh the stronger he becomes. He's moving all across the board freely setting up his pieces. You are no match for him. You need all the *help* you can get."

"Why did Jordin's mother have her committed?"

"Because a jealous Leviathan inhabits her."

"Lilith, from the garden. Where has she been hiding all of these millenniums upon millenniums?"

"Don't know. All I know is she's pissed. She has it out for Adriana and Jordin. Hell has no fury like a woman scorned."

"That doesn't make any sense. She's Satan's wife. Why would she be pissed about anything The Adversary is doing?"

"Ever since Satan was locked down in the black hole in the center of the Andromeda galaxy, she's been The Adversary's right hand. She thought they all were equal in power until Belial revealed she's beneath them all.

"Interesting."

"Isn't it? Things that make you say, 'hmmm'. She's the voice Adriana hears that tells her to kill Jordin."

"Really?"

"That's what she just told me. Leviathan uses a child's voice when she speaks to her. You know that's her signature."

Michael paused deep in thought. He scratched his closely shaved head, "Jordin, where is she?"

"St. Mary's. You better get there before he does. Now if you'll excuse me. I have a soul to save from eternal damnation and from a scorned fallen one."

Michael smiled, "Belie, the angel of unwavering love and devotion."

Belie stared at Michael through Ayana stunned. He paused remembering his old position.

Michael continued, "Fallen or not. You're still the angel of unwavering love and devotion to me brother. I sincerely thank you." Michael smiled.

Belie smiled through Ayana, "Go. You're running out of time. Pretty soon he'll be calling checkmate."

CHAPTER THIRTY

Michael walked through St. Mary's Behavioral Health facility in a hurry; his footsteps heavy and gritty. He went towards the front desk but no one was there. He stood for a minute looking around for someone, anyone that could tell him which room Jordin was in. A woman in her mid-50's approached the front desk. Her long dark brown hair with a hint of dark gray, dry in appearance, moved slightly as she moved in a hurry. Her white shoes squeaked across the extremely clean multi-colored tile floor as she said, "May I help you?"

Michael gave his usual bright smile as he said, "Jordin Reynolds's room please."

"Where is your coat? It's freezing out there?"

"Yes it is."

The woman peered up at him; "Are you a relative?"

Michael humbly smiled. The woman stared at him then grabbed a pen from the container on the desk and said, "You must be", she handed him the black ink pen then continued, "I need you to sign in on the clipboard, and I need a picture I.D."

Michael glanced at the clipboard sitting towards his left on the desk. He signed his name as Michael Reynolds because he did not have a last name. As he handed her the pen, "I don't have an I.D. I didn't know it was required. This is my first time visiting someone in a place like this. I walked from a long distance to get here."

She placed the pen in the container with the other pens, "Well, unfortunately it is policy. We keep your I.D. and return it to you on your way out the door."

"Ma'am please. Is there some exception? I *really* need to speak with her. It'll be quick I promise. Maybe you could walk me down and stand outside of the door or possibly have her come and speak with me right here in front of you. I came from near the university on foot."

The woman paused raising one eyebrow. She knew the university was way across town. She examined Michael from head to toe with her eyes. He didn't have on a coat so she knew that, not only did he come a long way, he nearly froze along the walk. She had pity for Michael and felt that he was genuine. As she stared at Michael, the armed security guard walked by on his way making his rounds. The woman said, "James, come here for a second please."

James, with his hand comfortably rested on his gun, slowly walked towards the front desk. He was the same height as Michael and about twenty pounds heavier with a military style haircut. He said, "Is there a problem?"

The woman said, "No, would you walk", she glanced at the clipboard then continued, "Michael down to little miss Reynold's room, Dr. Reynold's daughter?"

"Sure", James said.

"Thank you", Michael said feeling relieved.

The woman nodded her head as way of saying "you're welcome." Then she said, "Next time be sure to wear a coat…if you have one."

Michael smiled, "Yes ma'am."

As James and Michael walked down the long hallway, Michael glanced inside of the rooms that had opened doors. One elderly woman was sitting on her bed having a conversation with what appeared to be herself. Michael saw the fallen angel standing before her speaking with her. The spirit glanced at Michael while smirking. Michael shook his head in disapproval because that elderly woman had been committed to a mental health facility when a fallen one was actually speaking to her. Michael asked James, "Do you think all of these people are truly crazy?"

"I don't know and really don't care. All I can say is I feel bad for most of them."

"How so?"

"Some of them cry wanting to go home", he shook his head in disapproval then continued, "Others believe some entity is haunting them. It's truly sad sometimes. Makes me wonder with how long some people have been here if what they're saying could be true. I mean meds aren't working for them neither is any therapy."

Michael wanted so badly to tell James the truth that the spirit realm was real and the fallen ones possessed people even in this day and age. They actually spoke to people and showed themselves to people, but he feared he would be committed as well. Michael hung his head down and said, "You have a point. I just don't understand how anyone could believe someone could become insane overnight. I don't think Jordin is insane at all. I think mom is overreacting. Jordin doesn't belong here."

"I thought the same thing when I first saw her. Gorgeous she is, and upon talking to her, she doesn't seem crazy at all. But hey, they have the PhD's. Who am I to tell them how to do their job?"

They both approached the last door at the end of the hallway on the right. The door was opened as James said, "Here you go. I'll be standing right out here to give you two a *little* privacy."

"Thank you", Michael said then he walked in.

Inside the room, Jordin lain on her stomach with her arms folded in front of her like a pillow facing the thick Plexiglas window. She wore a white baggy t-shirt, some gray sweat pants, and a pair of white gym socks. Her hair was in a large braid down the middle of her head.

Michael knocked on the opened door, "Jordin?"

Jordin turned her head towards him as her mouth slightly opened. She sighed as she jumped up and ran to him embracing him with a hug with her head rested on his shoulder. Upon hugging him tears swelled in her eyes as she said, "Please tell me you're here to take me home."

Michael embraced her in return, "Unfortunately, no."

Jordin pulled away from him in disappointment. She hung her head down as she sat on the edge of her bed, "Then why are you here?"

Michael walked closer to the bed and knelt before Jordin whispering so James could not hear, "Sonya is still missing, and I need to find those trumpets."

Jordin raised an eyebrow, "Trumpets?" She stared up at the ceiling thinking then continued, "You talking about those antique trumpets that's been in their family like forever?"

"Yes, those. Sonya was going to show me where they were. They were keeping them for me. I'm running out of time and *really* need to get those trumpets as soon as possible."

"Well, I can't help you with that. The only person I know besides Sonya that would know anything about them would be Granna Nathan."

"Who is she?"

"Sonya's paternal grandmother, but she's in the hospital the last I heard. She's within her last days according to Sonya."

"Do you know which hospital?"

"Greene Memorial, room 4511."

Michael happily embraced her, "Oh thank you", he paused staring at the sad expression on her face then continued, "I know you're not crazy. I will do my best to get you out of here. Do not go to sleep tonight. Wait for me by this window."

Jordin glanced at the window. She snickered, "That window is like an inch thick and it's both bullet and shatter proof. Trust, I know personally when I threw a wooden chair into it and the chair broke without leaving a scratch on that damn window."

Michael smiled his usual bright smile, "Have a little faith."

Jordin grinned nodding her head in approval.

CHAPTER THIRTY ONE

Beliah strode down the street near Jones' Temple as the day approached nightfall. The colors of the sky reminded him of an abstract painting. When he stared at the canvas of the sky, he could see a clear picture, a picture that only he could see and understand. The scattered clouds seemed to make a face, the face of The Son with angels dancing around him. Beliah smiled then sighed.

As he walked, he observed his surroundings. Unlike other fallen ones, Beliah didn't like to simply appear then disappear he preferred to walk so he could see everything that surrounded him. Although Beliah once hated humans, he had a new understanding of their natures and a new sense of pity for some of them. He knew humans were receiving the greatest deception known through false religions and false perceptions of reality. He secretly wished he could show them the truth of things but knew he could not interfere with their free will. As a fallen one, the most he could do was try to influence or persuade them by possessing someone close to them which is something he had been doing for quite some time.

Beliah knew he was taking a huge risk in trying to locate Sonya for Michael, but he had a feeling, The Adversary desired more than simply using her to lure Michael to him. He feared the worst and wanted to stop The Adversary from accomplishing his mission. He knew he was stepping into dangerous territory that could hold dangerous consequences for him, but he did not care. He would rather die fighting for what's right than to die simply as a deceived fallen one.

As he approached Jones' Temple, Jaie, a fallen one hopelessly devoted to The Adversary appeared before him. Beliah smirked with sarcasm. Jaie said, "He's been expecting you." Beliah said, "So? Ooooh, I'm so afraid."

Jaie giggled, "You should be. Why don't you leave and spare yourself the shame."

"The moment I followed him gave me enough shame to last an eternity. You can't shame someone who's already ashamed."

Jaie tapped Beliah's shoulder, "Ah, come on. You know deep down inside you love it. This freedom."

Beliah snarled, "This is bondage."

Jaie shook his head in disapproval, "What happened to you? You were so thrilled expecting this kingdom."

"I *never* desired *this* kingdom. I was deceived and so were you, but you're too blind and too in love with him to see it."

Jaie frowned, "Watch it."

Beliah clinched his fists tightly, "You're no match for me and you know it. Back up boy."

As he stepped out of Beliah's way, Jaie said, "And you're no match for him, hmmm?"

Beliah pushed Jaie as he walked by, "Keep talking and I'll be back to kick your ass."

Jaie smirked then disappeared. Beliah knew he went to alert The Adversary of his presence. Beliah shook his head in disapproval. Every fallen one was devoted to The Adversary either out of fear or an odd sense of admiration and respect. In contrast, Beliah did not fear him nor respect him. He was in a class all by himself and a loner as he walked the earth as punishment for his sins.

Pastor Jones stood in the doorway of the church as Beliah approached. He crossed his arms and smirked as he leaned his left shoulder against the frame of the door. Beliah walked up the five steps of the church peering down at him, his eyebrows heavy and low. Pastor Jones said, "Beliah, not quite the surprise. Come on in. Let us converse for a spell."

Beliah glanced around the church frowning, "Hmmm, I don't feel welcomed in any house of yours."

Pastor Jones giggled, "Beliah displeased. Not a surprise. What can I do to make you feel welcomed?"

"Nothing. If you want to speak with me, do it right here."

"Very well then."

The Adversary stepped out of Pastor Jones as Pastor Jones shook his head trying to regain his thoughts. The Adversary turned to Pastor Jones and said, "Stay put. You will want to see this." Pastor Jones stood inside of the doorway in silence.

Beliah clinched his fists tightly as he stepped down the stairs backwards. The Adversary followed him down into the yard, "I hear you have been helping them. Yes?"

"Helping who?"

"Them. I knew you were up to something. I don't understand why you will not simply accept the decision you made. You cannot earn your way back into the heavens."

"Who said I wanted to?"

The Adversary paused in a brief moment of silence. He raised his left eyebrow and clinched his teeth together. He walked in a slow circle around Beliah as Beliah walked with him remaining face forward. The Adversary said, "Thwart my plan?"

"You lose."

"Funny you say that. I have the trumpet and soon to have the other."

Beliah smirked, "So arrogant you're stupid. I'm not talking about that. I guess you didn't know. Jordin is pregnant with Jensen's seed."

The Adversary laughed uproariously holding his stomach. He stopped laughing, staring at Beliah then he started laughing again, "You fool still as blind as before maybe even more so. I already have Darkness. I've always had her."

Beliah paused in a state of shock, "You're messing with my head."

"I assure you I am not. Jordin was a distraction, decoy if you will. Her seed is the supporter of my seed."

"Not if I can help it."

The Adversary back-handed Beliah with so much force he spinned with his head almost hitting the ground. Beliah opened his hand as a silver spear appeared. The Adversary opened his hand as his trident appeared. As he gripped the trident in a combative manner, "Shall we dance?"

They both encircled each other staring intently into each other's eyes. The Adversary said, "Your move."

Beliah rebuttaled, "After you."

The Adversary swung his trident as Beliah deflected with his spear. As he swung the trident, The Adversary spinned swinging the trident from over his shoulder trying to stab Beliah. Beliah swung his spear at the trident in an attempt to knock it down as he jumped back to prevent himself from being jabbed. The Adversary smirked as he stabbed at Beliah again and again backing him all the way towards the street. Pastor Jones stared in both amazement and fear.

The Adversary swung his trident upwards almost striking Beliah in his chin.

Beliah jumped back into the street as cars passing by drove directly through him. The Adversary spread his wings flying towards Beliah with his trident pointed towards him. Beliah stood bracing himself for the collision as he rapidly twirled the spear in a circle as a shield. The Adversary collided with Beliah with his trident aimed at Beliah's chest. Beliah's spear knocked the trident down causing him to be stabbed in his right thigh instead of his chest knocking him across the street into a tree as The Adversary held onto him. The Adversary yanked his trident out of Beliah's thigh preparing to finish him, but he moved in slow motion. No matter what he tried he could not move within real time.

A bright light shone around both Beliah and The Adversary blinding the both of them as they both covered their eyes. Beliah without a second thought knelt down on one knee and bowed his head. The Adversary appeared frightened dropping his trident and taking a few steps back. The Son appeared before the both of them so bright he was simply a blotch of light without form. The Son said, "Cease!"

The Adversary shielding his face said, "It's not your time yet. Does The Father break his own rules now?"

The Son said, "I do not answer to you. Beliah, you requested a meeting."

Beliah said, "Yes."

The Son said, "Come with me The Father and The Elders are awaiting."

Beliah said, "Thank you." He stood walking towards The Son with a serious limp.

The Adversary stared at Beliah angrily, "You have to return. We'll finish this, yes?"

The Son said, "This will only be finished at judgment."

The Adversary said, "You think you have influence, power perhaps? You have nothing. These humans do not know you, seek you, believe in you, nor submit to you. Let us be honest here. Do you truly love them or is it required for you to love them?"

The Son approached The Adversary. The Adversary struggled not to kneel to him, but could not stop himself. He knelt and bowed his head. The Son said, "You have no comprehension of love. This is meaningless, and I refuse to entertain you."

The Son took Beliah by his hand as they vanished. The Adversary stood to his feet as his eyebrows grumbled and his nose flared. He turned towards where Pastor Jones stood in the doorway. He was gone.

CHAPTER THIRTY TWO

Michael stood in front of room 4511. The door was cracked as nurses walked up and down the hallway with some entering and exiting patient rooms. Some of them nodded and smiled at him as others greeted him. Michael smiled and nodded in return and verbally greeted the ones that greeted him. Michael lightly knocked on the door as he crept into the room slowly not to startle anyone.

Inside of the room, the curtain was pulled covering the entire bed. The blinds covering the window were cracked as a bit of sunlight shown through. The restroom door was opened with the light on and the sounds of the game show on the television filled the silence of the room. Michael said, "Hello, Mrs. Nathan, are you there?"

Granna Nathan, her voice raspy and deep, said, "It's Granna Nathan."

Michael crept to the curtain said, "May I please have a word with you?"

"Pull the curtain back and have a seat."

Michael pulled the curtain back as Granna Nathan turned the light on above the bed. She was a small, frail looking woman. No more than five feet tall and appeared to be around 90lbs. She had long white hair that almost touched her behind and had a youthful appearance. She was 95 years old but didn't look a day over 70. Granna Nathan motioned for Michael to sit in the chair underneath the wall the television posted and said, "Where in the world is your coat son? It's freezing out there. You know good and well you're not used to this."

As Michael sat, "It was damaged."

Granna Nathan leaned back crossing her arms, "Or perhaps you never had one." She chuckled.

Michael stared at Granna Nathan examining her with his eyes. She appeared healthy and only had an I.V. in her left arm. He said, "How have you been?"

"Dying. Looking forward to seeing everyone again. Glad to be leaving this wicked, wicked world. It's my time son. Been sitting here waiting on you."

"Waiting on me?"

"I know exactly who you are, what you want, and what this time is."

Michael smiled, "Do you know where Sonya is?"

"With him."

"Pastor Jones?"

"When you were busy battling. The real Pastor Jones crept in, took her by her hand, and said, 'Come with me.' My poor baby was so afraid she left with him."

Michael leaned up in the chair, "How do you now this?"

"True revelation comes from Yah. I was blessed to be born with gifts and so was my eldest granddaughter."

"What do you mean?"

"Divine revelation. We were put here on this earth for this very special purpose. I will not go home until my purpose is fulfilled. Hahaha! Halleluiah!"

Michael smiled, "I know that's right. So where is Sonya?"

"You don't worry about that son. You will see her soon and so will I."

Michael lowered his head, "I saw the news. I'm so sorry about your son."

Granna Nathan bit down on her lip and turned the television off, "Thank you. I knew the night before. I prayed and I prayed for the strength. I knew when my boy was a child that Adversary would come for him. He had dreams similar to Sonya."

"And the trumpets?"

"I'm afraid son that Adversary took one of the trumpets."

Michael sighed in disappointment, "Do you know where the other one is."

"Why yes I do. See, I had a vision a decade ago that he would kill my son and take the both of them", she tapped her temple region then continued, "But I got smart. I buried the other trumpet the very day I buried my Gregory. He is holding onto it in his casket."

"That was smart of you."

"Yes I know."

Michael paused. He stared into thin air thinking. He knew once he had the trumpet he would have to face The Adversary in order to get the other. He didn't know if he had the strength left in his flesh to fight him and his legions. He knew it would not be a one on one battle and then he thought about his promise to Jordin. He also thought about Sonya. He had an eerie feeling. He said, "Where is his grave?"

"He's buried under the name Robert Willis at Jefferson Cemetery."

Zest stood in the restroom listening to their entire conversation.

CHAPTER THIRTY THREE

The non-possessed Pastor Jones stood in the basement of Jones' Temple in the doorway of one of the rooms. Sonya lain in the twin sized bed obviously drugged. Her hair was curly and wild upon her head, her eyes droopy and low, with a bandage on her leg. Her scars, cuts, and scrapes were healing well. There was a bucket next to the bed to catch any vomit that she may expel.

The room was dim due to the black lamp shade with a small amount of light coming in from the two small windows due to the sun setting. The bed appeared comfortable and she was kept warm with a nice green, gold, and maroon satin comforter. She wore a red sweat suit and white socks appearing clean despite her wild hair. Pastor Jones said, "It's time to go." He grabbed her arm pulling her to sit up. She sat up, but he could tell she was dizzy from the morphine injections the possessed Pastor Jones gave her for the pain of her injuries from the attack in the alley. Those injections kept her high enough so not to escape. Sonya mumbled, "What are you doing? Where are you taking me?"

As Pastor Jones, put her socks on her, "I'm getting you out of here. You don't need to be here. I don't know why he is keeping you here when you're not dreaming anymore."

"I feel sick."

"Of course you do. He's been drugging you. That isn't medicine he's been giving you."

"What? Why are you talking about yourself in second person?"

It wasn't me. He is evil, the very definition of. All of these years I have doubted but it's real. Everything is real. The Father…everything is too real."

"What are you talking about? He? You're the only person who's been taking care of me."

"I know it's hard for you to understand right now but that was not me. It was him."

"Who is him?"

As he put her shoes on her and tied then up, "The Adversary. It's time for us to go."

The Adversary appeared as a bright light that diffused immediately. Sonya's eyes bulged slightly. He stood on the other side of Sonya's bed near the wall across from the door. His eyebrows crumbled as he said, "What do you think you are doing?"

Pastor Jones said, "She needs to go home. She's not dreaming anymore. What do you think you are doing?"

"Watch it or you be digesting your own testicles."

Pastor Jones smirked, "You actually think you strike fear in me. You need me."

The Adversary screamed in rage sounding like a lion's roar as he approached

Pastor Jones, "Need you. I need no one you arrogant bastard."

"Then kill me. Whatever you do to me I don't care anymore. I'm already hell bound off of the things I allowed you to make me do. All I know is she's going home." Pastor Jones picked Sonya up and carried her out of the room. As they walked towards the basement steps, The Adversary said, "That is the plan. I, or should I say, we are going to take her home."

Pastor Jones turned to him, "What are you up to? What is your purpose with her? You've killed her father, you've killed her mother, you've raped her friend; what else is there for you to do to her? Leave her be."

"Of all the women you have played with and used including your own wife, you have fallen for her, yes? Do you love her Billy, hmmm? From the moment you saw her, you wanted her. Broke your neck to give her that bible with your number on the back page. Tried desperately to get close to her so you could get her to join your congregation. You desired her so much you couldn't wait to rescue her."

"I'm not doing this with you," Pastor Jones turned and continued towards the steps.

"Sonya, did you know your friend Billy murdered your beloved pastor and had a year-long affair with your good friend Adriana? See, I'm not the only one that cannot be trusted."

Sonya said, "It's not true. You lie."

The Adversary said, "How about it Billy? Am I making this up?"

Pastor Jones put Sonya down on the steps where she sat sideways struggling to hold her head up. He turned to The Adversary and said, "You made me do it."

"You did it on your own free will. You had a choice and you chose to kill. You are officially mine."

"No, you coerced me. You used me. You did all of this you evil bastard."

"If I'm evil, what does that make you? Kind? I think not."

Pastor Jones had a blank expression on his face. The Adversary turned into black smoke and returned to Pastor Jones' body through his nostrils.

Sonya appeared horrified as she tried to climb up the stairs to get away from him. The Adversary said to her as he slowly approached her, "Do not be afraid. I am taking you to Michael. I promise you will get to him unscathed. Have I hurt you thus far?" he gently grabbed her leg to prevent her from crawling up the stairs.

Sonya's heart beat hastened as her palms sweated. She stopped trying to escape, turned to him, and said, "No."

"And I will not. I have kept you safe. Have the fallen ones bothered you since you have been here?"

"No."

"You can trust that I will not harm you," the possessed Pastor Jones gently picked Sonya up carrying her back to the room, "You rest now, and I will take you to see Michael later on tonight. After that, you will never have to worry about seeing me again."

KENERLY PRESENTS

CHAPTER THIRTY FOUR

Jordin sat in the chair near the window. The day had turned into night as she could see her reflection and the reflection of the room in the large window as well as see the trees and grass outside. The hospital had a large campus and was full of trees, bushes, and grass; right off of a street near the freeway. She was fully dressed waiting on Michael as she spoke to Adriana.

Adriana sat on the edge of Jordin's bed with her coat still on and her gloves in her right hand. She had on some leather knee high boots without a heel. She sat with her legs crossed and her hair hidden under a wool cap.

Jordin said, "And that's what Ayana told you?"

"Yes. She said Pastor Jones is The Adversary."

Jordin ran her hands across her head from forehead to back, dropped them into her lap then said, "I don't know. Shit's been too weird. Momma is not behaving like momma. I don't know who the fuck that bitch is anymore. Fuck 'em. My brain just can't take trying to rationalize this shit."

"Well, I need to. I need to know if Pastor Jones is really Pastor Jones."

Jordin stared at Adriana squinting her eyes, "Why do you care so much? If he is The Adversary, just stop going to his church. Problem solved."

Adriana stood and slowly walked towards the window peering out, "I wish it was that simple."

"I'm lost. What do you mean? It is that simple. Stop going to his church. That's how you stay away from him."

"Did you hear about Jensen?"

"No. What about him?"

"He broke into Mr. Nathan's house and Mr. Nathan killed him."

Jordin took in a deep hard swallow. Although she didn't like to admit it or show it, she had feelings for him, "Damn."

"Yeah", Adriana turned and walked towards Jordin. She sat on the corner of Jordin's chair with her back towards her, "I'm pregnant."

Jordin lowered her head, "So am I."

Adriana turned towards Jordin, "When did you find out? How far along?"

"I found out this morning, and I'm seven weeks along."

"By who? Roger? Bryce? Jermaine?"

Jordin paused as she wiped her eye, "I don't know. It's between them and two more guys; too close to pinpoint for sure. My mom is gonna have a field's day with this."

Adriana's mouth opened wide, "Oh my."

"Yeah, but truth be told I don't want this baby. I'm not having this baby. I have to get the fuck up out of here." Jordin stood, walked to the bed, and sat on it. Adriana slid into her spot in the chair. Jordin said, "I can feel in my soul that this baby is evil. I have never in my life been attracted to him." She raised her left eyebrow, "Then suddenly we're fucking? Nah that fat fucker put a spell on me. For me to actually be sad that he's dead? I've been hexed."

"I don't believe that. In order for you to be hexed you have to believe in that stuff. You don't believe in it. You don't believe in anything."

"That was the pre-haunted Jordin. You'd be surprised what I believe now."

"Well, I don't believe you were hexed. Maybe somewhere along the line, you fell for him. You were one of the only people in school that spoke to him and hung out with him. Pity can keep you longer than love and pity can make you think you love someone."

Jordin shook her slowly, "I don't know. All I know is I don't want this damn baby."

"What about giving it up for adoption?"

"I'm not having this baby, okay? Besides while we're discussing me, how far along are you and who knocked you up miss virgin?"

Adriana smirked, "I never told you I was a virgin. That was your assumption because I wouldn't sleep with the lames you hooked me up with. And before I say a word you have to promise me on your life you won't tell anyone."

"Come on now. This is me."

Adriana raised her right eyebrow, "Promise me."

"I promise."

"Ten weeks and its Pastor Jones'"

Jordin's eyes bulged as she jumped up in the bed onto her knees, "Shut up."

"I'm serious. He and I have been messing around for the past six months."

"I never would have thought you would have an affair with a married man."

"I tried to tell you I wasn't a saint."

"Do you want the baby?"

"Of course I do. Who wouldn't want a baby by a man that fine?"

"Even if he is The Adversary?"

Adriana paused, "Nothing in this world could make me to kill this baby. I'm having him or her and I suggest you have yours too. I'll just pray about it. If he or she is evil, I'll still love it anyway."

Jordin snickered, "That's all you 'cause I wouldn't be able to love baby Lucifer. Tiny evil ass be strangling other babies 'cause they won't give him they pacifiers and shit", she giggled.

Adriana giggled, "You're silly, but seriously, I don't know. I'm just gonna pray about it and it is what it is."

"You haven't told him yet have you?"

"No, I've been avoiding him since I found out. I wonder if he will be mad."

"If I were him, I would be. This baby exposes him for who he truly is. No true man of God cheats on his wife."

"You of all people can't say that. Besides, how do you know what a man of God should and should not do? You cringe at the sight of a bible so it isn't like you've actually read it. I distinctly remember you telling me that you can't go to church because as soon as your foot touches the ground you'd melt."

Jordin giggled, "Yeah, I did say that didn't I? But things are different now."

"Even so, we all fall short and he is human. Men of God aren't perfect because they're still men."

"That's true but still."

Michael stood at the window tapping on it. Jordin turned her attention to the window. When she saw Michael, she gave a big smile, and ran to the window.

CHAPTER THIRTY FIVE

Pastor Jones sat in his home office wearing a light long sleeve button down shirt with his black slacks sharply creased. His hair pulled back into a neat ponytail and his face perfectly shaved as he attempted to grow a goatee. His left elbow rested against the top of the cherry wood desk as he slightly leaned upon it. His other hand rested on the mouse as he stared at the computer screen. He searched through the obituary of the local newspaper trying to find the obituary of Gregory Nathan. His eyes peered around the desktop computer screen at Sonya lying across the black leather loveseat. Her hair pulled back into a neat ponytail as she slept peacefully.

Zest appeared to him standing next to the window in the corner adjacent to where Pastor Jones sat. The light from the lamp on Pastor Jones desk was dim so the corners of the room appeared dark. Pastor Jones said, "What is it you need?"

Zest stared at Sonya, "What is she doing here? What will your wife say?"

"I have no wife other than the beautiful Semiramis." The possessed Pastor Jones sighed then continued, "Who is sleeping until that great and dreadful day."

"Well, what will Pastor Jones' wife say about her?"

"Frankly, I care not."

"I've heard your son will be born in August; a Leo, the great lion."

"My only son is the great and powerful Nimrod the only person that believed in my vision and executed it. That child is Pastor Jones'."

"I don't understand."

"I entered her through him by means of a ritual. Her son is a goblin. His purpose is to follow my instruction. He is all human. He is not a nephilim. My only son was taken from me. Instead of walking the earth to be by my side, he is in the abyss."

Zest, still remaining among the dark corner of the room, said, "They're together."

Pastor Jones clicked the mouse to go the next obituary, "Who is they?"

"Michael. He used the last bit of his powers to break Jordin out of the hospital."

"Good. He will be that much easier to dispatch."

"But there's more."

Pastor Jones peered from in front of the computer monitor, "Go on."

"Adriana is with him."

Pastor Jones' eyes crumbled. He licked his lips then rubbed down his beard with his hand cuffed over his mouth. He pressed the power button on the computer monitor then stood walking towards Zest. He mumbled to himself aloud, "What are you up to Michael?" He stared at Zest, "Does he know?"

"I don't think so."

"We must find them. I have to protect that seed at all costs. Not a hair on Adriana's head will be touched. Make sure as many fallen ones as you can find cover her."

"I know where they are headed."

"Where?"

"Jefferson Cemetery."

Pastor Jones glanced at Sonya smirking.

CHAPTER THIRTY SIX

The moon was full without hardly any clouds upon the sky. The glow made the surrounding sky appear a diffused purplish-blue as the rest of the sky appeared mid-night blue, so dark it almost appeared black. The stars shone brilliantly scattered appearing like tiny glistening gemstones in the sky. Michael, Adriana, and Jordin walked along the street in the bitter cold. The temperature that night was two degrees but the wind chill made it feel like it was well below zero. Adriana was the only person wearing a coat as Jordin and Michael walked along holding each other trying to keep warm from each other's body heat.

Michael noticed a car parked along the street. There was a red, four door neon parked at a meter. The traffic was still that night, not many cars passed along the street going to and from. Michael stopped causing Adriana and Jordin to stop as well. He said, "I have an idea."

Jordin said, "Are you thinking what I'm thinking?"

Michael smiled, "It depends on what you're thinking."

Jordin said, "Watch and learn my friend. As a teenager, stealing cars was my specialty."

Jordin approached the car. She stared into the window at the inside then she turned to Adriana and said, "Your purse."

Adriana handed Jordin her purse. Jordin took out a pocket knife. She handed the purse back to Adriana. Jordin stuck the sharp blade of the pocket knife against the corner of the lock. Michael said, "What are you doing?"

Jordin said, "Wait and see."

Michael said, "But…"

Jordin cut him off, "I got this."

Jordin hit it a few times then went around the lock hitting and pulling. She stuck the knife into a corner then pulled the knife handle towards her popping the lock out of socket. Michael smirked. He said, "You didn't have to go through all of that". He pulled a straight key out of his pocket.

Adriana shook her head in disapproval, "Both of y'all are so simple." Adriana walked into the street towards the passenger side door, opened it then said, "The fucking car isn't locked."

Jordin had a dumbfounded expression on her face. Michael smiled, "Well okay then."

Michael climbed into the driver seat and ripped open the steering column to wire the car. Adriana climbed into the passenger seat. Jordin folded the pocket knife, slid it on her pocket then climbed in the back seat behind Michael. Once he got the car started, Michael closed the car door then pulled off.

Jordin said, "First stop my house, so I can pack a bag and get the hell out of dodge."

Michael said, "No. First stop is the sporting goods store. I need a shovel, a golf bag, a hand gun, and a net."

Adriana frowned, "What do you need all of that for?"

"We're going to the cemetery."

Adriana said, "The hell I am. Let me out."

Jordin said, "Calm down girl."

"Calm down? This nigga trying to kill us."

Michael said, "I am not. I'm going to the cemetery to dig up a treasure. I will not harm you. You have my word."

Jordin said, "Adriana, you can trust him. We can trust him. Stop fretting."

Adriana turned to look at Jordin, "Give me my knife."

Jordin pulled the pocket knife out of her pocket then handed it to Adriana. Adriana snatched the knife and said, "Thank you." She turned around in her seat facing forward then said, "I don't know why, but I have a bad feeling about this. Jordin you're a mental health fugitive, I'm your accomplice, and we just stole someone's car."

Jordin said, "If they catch me, I will tell them you had nothing to do with it. You were my hostage."

Adriana turned around to look at Jordin, "How can we explain a bullet proof window pulled out of the frame? Did you not see? The window is missing. I just wanna be let out."

Michael said, "Where would you go?"

Adriana said, "I don't know and I don't care. This is too much drama for me. All I care about is remaining calm so I can have this baby."

Michael said, "You're pregnant?"

Jordin said, "Yep, and so am I."

Michael's mouth opened wide as he remembered speaking with Sonya. He thought back to her dream:

Sonya flew away landing on a tall mountain as Elijah pointed to the sky, peering up at heaven while it stood open. As heaven opened, a rider on a white horse headed down whose name was Faithful and true, with eyes like blazing fire, and he had many crowns on his head. He was dressed in a robe that had been dipped in blood and his name was the Word of God. Then Elijah pointed down to the earth and Sonya saw a beast come up from the abyss with two horns like a lamb, but he spoke like a great dragon. He exercised all the authority of the first beast, whose fatal wound had healed, and this beast had the face of Pastor Jones.

Michael gasped as he had a vision.

INTERLUDE

Thirty one years into the future Pope John Paul III whose birth name was William Jones, Jr. sat in his chair with a golden cup in his hand. The ecumenical movement was moving full force, the world was transitioning towards new world religion and new world government, and Pope John Paul III was chosen to head the new world religion as the youngest pope in history; half Caucasian and half Columbian looking exactly like Pastor Jones but with dark brown hair and green eyes.

The chosen head of the new world government was Jason Reynolds; half African American and half Caucasian who was born and raised in the city of the second beast. He was the youngest American president and the first world leader. Charming, charismatic, with a powerful speaking voice, he sat to the left of Pope John Paul III at the world headquarters in the city of Jerusalem. The third temple's construction was almost complete.

Pope John Paul III resided in the city called the first beast, drunk with the blood of the saints whose city sat among seven hills, but was born of the city of the second beast. His city was a harlot that fornicated with the nations by blending heathenism with truth creating a religion that was a complete abomination and mockery. The Vatican was the appointed headquarters of the new world religion.

The depopulation plans were in effect as wars continued to rage, the government controlled the weather, and modern medications and vaccines poisoned the people of the world. All of the world leaders came together at the new world council meeting to discuss methods to speed up the depopulation process.

Pope John Paul III said, "We must murder all professing Christians, Muslims, and Jews. We are in a new aeon with a new religion. We cannot tolerate these feeble belief systems. They halt our evolution. We are on the verge of a powerful paradigm shift. We are evolving into higher, more powerful beings through our consciousness. These fools are keeping us in the stone-age. We must rid them and their followers. We are gods, and it's about time we start thinking, believing, and behaving as such."

The council members cheered and clapped uproariously. Jason Reynolds stood and said, "The pope is right. If these simpletons do not join us they are against us and they must die. It is our right to be who we are, we are little gods, and gods are not weak. The weak must die. The sick must die. The weak and sick are like diseases that we cannot afford to keep around. Sick people create other sick people. Weak people create other weak people. We cannot have that in our genome.

This is the time. The time is now. We must have one last major world war. Through war and natural disasters, that is how we speed up the process. We cause tsunamis of biblical proportions, earthquakes, hurricanes, and drought. This last world war must be the grandest of wars."

The council members cheered loudly, clapping, whistling, and gave a standing ovation as Jason returned to his seat. Pope John Paul III stood and said, "We continue putting diseases and harmful substances such as mercury and aluminum in vaccines. We continue putting fluorine in the drinking water, etc. We continue dumbing down the education system and keeping them distracted by means of entertainment, sex, and drugs, so they remain oblivious to our plan. We continue crashing the world's economy so they have no choice but to lean towards us begging and hanging on our every word. We continue to threaten the safety of their families with terrorist threats and famine. We make them believe killing each other is the only means of their survival. We continue. We continue."

Jason Reynolds smiled, stood, and clapped for the pope. He raised his hand to the crowd of world leaders as they cheered and clapped for him.

CHAPTER THIRTY SEVEN

Pastor Jones pulled up on a side street close to the cemetery with Sonya sitting in the passenger seat. His style of dress was relaxed as he wore a pair of winter boots, a pair of jeans, a multi-colored sweater, and a thick dark green coat. He wore thick cotton gloves and a wool hat; the complete opposite of his typical professional style of dress.

Sonya sat with a hint of nervousness on her face. He took really good care of her, but he was possessed by The Adversary himself. She secretly wondered what was in store for her. She wondered why he was so nice to her. She didn't know someone so evil could be so nice. As a result, she did not trust him but was afraid that if she challenged him in any way that he would kill her. She prayed and prayed, and knew her prayers had been answered because he had yet to harm her in any way. She stared at the starry night sky recalling one of her favorite scriptures: "The heavens declare the glory of God; the skies proclaim the work of his hands. Day after day they pour forth speech; and night after night they reveal knowledge." Sonya thought to herself, *I'm listening. What are you trying to tell me?"*

Pastor Jones turned the truck off and snatched the keys out of the ignition. Sonya turned to him and said, "Did you really give me Heroine?"

Pastor Jones smiled, "A derivative called Morphine. Did it not help with the pain?"

"Yes, it did…Thank you."

Pastor Jones frowned leaning away from Sonya, "For what?"

"For being so good to me when you could have killed me."

Pastor Jones' eyebrows crumbled. He did not like the thought of doing anything "good". He opened the door then said, "I could have yet I could not. Time to go."

He climbed out of the truck. Sonya opened the door but remained seated. Pastor Jones grabbed her metal crutches from the bed of his truck then handed them to her. During the battle in the alley, the poltergeist broke Sonya's leg when he hit her with the wooden stick. The non-possessed Pastor Jones ran into the alley, rescued her, and took her to the emergency department. He convinced her to stay with him so he could protect her before The Adversary re-inhabited his body. The Adversary planned that attack, and because of the information he received from Zest, knew exactly where they were and what they were doing.

Sonya grabbed the crutches and got out of the truck. She leaned against the crutches for a few seconds because the morphine was wearing off and the pain was returning. She had a broken leg and three broken ribs on the left side of her ribcage. The bruises and scratches on her face and body were healing but remained noticeable. The bite on her shoulder appeared as though it might leave a nasty scar as she needed one hundred and seventy five stitches to mend her torn flesh. She lost so much blood that she needed a blood transfusion; he bit her almost to the bone.

She gripped the hand rests of the crutches tightly as she hobble behind Pastor Jones towards the rear of the truck. Pastor Jones grabbed a long black duffle bag from the bed of the truck and slung the straps over his right shoulder. He zipped his coat up all the way until it stopped close to his neck. He peered up at the full moon then glanced at Sonya. He said, "Shall we?"

Sonya asked, "Where are we going?"

"To the grave of Robert Willis."

"Why?"

"This is the place we will make the exchange."

"What exchange?"

Pastor Jones smirked, "You for the other trumpet."

Sonya took in a deep hard swallow, "What if he doesn't give it to you?"

Pastor Jones raised his left eyebrow, "Then you have a serious problem."

CHAPTER THIRTY EIGHT

Jordin sat on the tombstone of Robert Willis as Michael stood inside of the grave shoveling dirt to the surface. His arms felt tired as he dug in, lifted up, and tossed dirt over his shoulder as fast as he could. He knew he had to get the trumpet as quick as possible. He felt in his bones that The Adversary was on his way to get the trumpet from him. Michael was aware that he could not beat him strength for strength, pound for pound. As he gripped the shovel before digging it into the earth, he tried to make his hands illuminate. His hands illuminated for a quick second then diffused. Michael was completely human and had no more otherworldly powers at his disposal. He attempted to stick the shovel into the earth but the shovel was stopped by the hardness of the pearl casket. Michael leaned down brushing dirt away revealing the top of Gregory's casket as he tossed the shovel up onto the pile of dirt that rested next to Adriana.

Adriana stood next to the opened grave moving dirt away from the opening. The golf bag leaned up against the tombstone with a portion resting upon Jordin's thigh. When Adriana saw the shovel, she said, "You reached it?"

Michael said, "Yes, this is it. You might want to back away. There's no telling how long this body has been in here. The smell alone could kill you."

Jordin stood catching the golf bag from falling. Michael said, "Jordin, the bag."

Jordin grabbed the golf bag then tossed it to Michael. She stared into the grave wanting to see the body inside. Adriana turned her back towards them because she did not want to see it. Michael straddled the coffin with each foot on each side pulling on the left side. He opened the coffin as he was nearly blinded by the shiny silver trumpet as it heavily reflected the light from the full moon.

Jordin covered her eyes a bit with her hand peeking between her fingers. Gregory lain there in a light blue suit with a salmon colored button down shirt underneath. His body had barely decomposed but the smell caused Michael to cover his nose.

Michael held his breath as he knelt down and picked up the almost three feet long keyless trumpet. The trumpet was engraved with ancient Hebrew lettering near the handle as the remainder of the trumpet was a smooth, polished silver. Michael was astonished at how light the trumpet was. With its length, he assumed it would have some weight to it, but it felt like it weighed a few ounces. Michael slid the trumpet into the golf bag then slung the straps of the bag over his left shoulder.

Jordin was tossed into a tree, smacked the tree backwards hitting her head against the bark. Her body slid down as she lain on the ground as if asleep. Adriana's eyes bulged as Pastor Jones placed his index finger to his lips to silently tell her to not say one word. Adriana stood frozen. Michael peered up noticing she appeared shocked and afraid. He reached his hand up grabbing onto the side of the grave to pull himself out. Pastor Jones stepped on his hand.

Michael said, "Ouch!" He let go removing his hand and shaking it.

Pastor Jones said, "Now, hand it to me."

Michael peered up out of the grave as Pastor Jones stood over him from atop, "Never."

Pastor Jones pulled Sonya next to him, "Not even for her?"

Michael lowered his head, sighed then said, "She has nothing to do with this. Please turn her loose. You are more powerful than I. How about we fight for it? Winner takes them."

Pastor Jones giggled as he laid the duffle bag onto the ground, "Michael, Michael...always something up your sleeve. That will not do. Hand me the trumpet or she dies."

Sonya peered at Pastor Jones, "You said you wouldn't harm me."

Pastor Jones snarled, "I lied."

Michael paused. He rubbed his eyes with his index finger and thumb. He peered up at the duffle bag hanging from Pastor Jones' shoulder, "Let me up."

"Hand me the trumpet first."

"No, you are not getting this trumpet until you let me up. Same time."

Pastor Jones laughed, "Do you not realize the predicament you are in? How dare you make demands? I could kill all of you right now and walk away with trumpet."

Michael pulled out his hand gun and pointed it at Adriana's head, "And I could kill her. She has something you desire more than this trumpet."

Pastor Jones' nose flared in anger wondering how Michael knew. He glanced at Adriana then back at Michael. Adriana appeared baffled then said, "Is it true? Are you Satan? Am I carrying the anti-Christ?"

Pastor Jones said, "There was a time when women were silenced," He grabbed Adriana by her throat, "It's about time we revert back to that. Speak when spoken to. Two men are talking," he pushed her as he released hold of her neck then peered at Michael, "You will not. I dare you."

Adriana grabbed her neck gasping. Michael glanced at Sonya. She stood six inches away from Pastor Jones directly next to him. Adriana stood four feet away from Pastor Jones and slightly behind him and he did not see Jordin at all. Michael said, "How about it brother? Let me up and fight me...unless you're still afraid."

Pastor Jones released a ferocious, ear splitting lion's roar. Both Sonya and Adriana covered their ears as the roar awakened Jordin. She rubbed her eyes feeling the pain from the impact. Pastor Jones said, "Afraid!...You should be afraid! I fear nothing, not you, not the son, not The Father!...I am...I am." His eyes flashed a deep red hue.

With one stare, Pastor Jones picked Michael up and flung him out of the grave. The golf bag slid off of his shoulder as he tumbled in the air. He landed on the ground on his side sliding into a headstone. The golf bag flung to the ground as the trumpet slid out of it and stopped next to Jordin. Michael held his gun steady pointed towards Adriana as he slowly stood. Pastor Jones grabbed a hold of Sonya's collar walking her towards Michael as she did not attempt to resist. He said, "You love her Michael?"

Michael glanced at Adriana, "Do you love her?"

Pastor Jones said, "You will not shoot nor kill her. Answer me. How much do you love these automatons?"

As Pastor Jones approached Michael, Jordin slowly pulled the trumpet towards her while pretending to still be knocked out. She noticed the duffle bag Pastor Jones had lying on the ground next to the grave. She devised a plan in her mind on how she would get the bag and get it to Michael.

Adriana stood frozen wondering if Michael would really shoot her. She never trusted Michael and did not believe he was really an archangel. She secretly wondered why the trumpets were so important.

Pastor Jones glanced at the trumpet lying next to Jordin then he stared at Michael, "See, I was going to make a fair exchange, Sonya for the trumpet, but you provoked me."

Jordin slowly and quietly pulled out a handgun from the inside of her sweat pants. She pointed it at Pastor Jones.

Jaie appeared shouting, "She has a gun!" Pastor Jones turned his head to look at Jordin but before he could look at her, she shot him in chest. He screamed reaching his hand out then closed it. Jordin's body snapped horizontally in half backwards. Sonya gasped as Michael shot him in his chest.

Pastor Jones stepped back still holding onto Sonya's collar. Sonya screamed, "Uriel!" Michael shot Pastor Jones in his chest again. Without hesitation, Pastor Jones reached his hand inside of Sonya's chest ripping out her heart. Still beating in his hand he tossed it at Michael. Michael screamed dodging the heart. Adriana screamed and ran away.

As she ran away, Adriana ran towards Jordin grabbing Jordin's gun as she continued on. When she passed a tree, Leviathan stepped

out as Adriana ran into her. Leviathan now
inhabited her body. As soon as Leviathan
entered, Adriana stopped running and turned
around to watch.

Sonya's body dropped to the ground at
the same time Uriel's feet touched the ground.
Uriel ran to her but she was lifeless. He bowed
his head in deep sadness as he closed her eyes
and mouth.

The Adversary's wings burst out of
Pastor Jones' back. He stepped out of Pastor
Jones as Pastor Jones' lifeless body dropped to
the ground. As The Adversary burst out of
Pastor Jones, Michael grabbed the trumpet next
to Jordin's body and blew it. The Adversary
and Jaie covered their ears because the sound
was so dreadful for the fallen ones.

Michael ran towards the duffle bag that
contained the other trumpet while keeping a
tight grip on the trumpet in his hand. The
Adversary pushed out his arm with his hand
opened blowing Michael into a head stone.
Michael flipped over the head stone as Uriel
stood watching. Uriel was not allowed to help
Michael unless The Adversary crossed the line.
As soon as Michael hit the ground, he blew the
trumpet again. The Adversary and Jaie
screamed as they covered their ears as in a great
amount of pain. Michael ran towards the duffle
bag, slid, and grabbed it. The possessed
Adriana stepped from behind a tree shooting

Michael seven times, five in the trunk of his body and two in his thigh.

Michael gasped for air as two bullets pierced his lungs. He felt every bit of the pain as he struggled to hang onto to his life. He dropped to his knees with the duffle bag in one hand and the trumpet in the other refusing to drop them again. He spit blood as Uriel walked towards him.

Adriana stood with the gun still pointed at Michael. She glanced at Pastor Jones' body then at The Adversary. She glanced at Sonya then Jordin. She peered up at the sky as it appeared to open then back at Michael. She shot Michael in his chest. Michael howled in pain. Uriel glanced at the gun as it was snatched out of her hand by an invisible force. Leviathan exited her body as Adriana stood frozen unaware of what just happened.

Michael coughed up and spit out some more blood. The Adversary went to Michael and said, "Any last words?" Michael spit up some blood as his lungs rattled when he breathed; he was suffocating in his own body. The Adversary placed one hand on each of Michael's shoulders, "You shame even me." He ripped Michael in half. Adriana vomited profusely from the sight. Uriel stared at The Adversary, "You satisfied? It's over."

The Adversary said, "Not until I say it is."

Uriel walked towards him combatively, "He's dead. It's over."

The Adversary said, "Enrages you doesn't it?"

Uriel smacked his lips together, "What do you mean?"

The Adversary smirked, "I won. Now move so I can get my trumpets."

Uriel moved out of his way while pointing at the trumpets, "You mean those trumpets?"

The duffle bag and the trumpet that was in Michael's hands had disappeared. The Adversary screamed tearing a tree up from the roots tossing it across the cemetery. He walked around in circles staring up at the opened sky beating on his chest, "So this is how you play? You cheat me. I knew you were not just and true. You are a fraud! I won. All of you saw it for yourselves. He was killed before he could take the trumpets to the heavens. I want my victory credited! I killed the Great Michael. I did! I did this."

Michael's human body disappeared as he dropped down from the heavens in his angelic form. He was the same height as The Adversary, 20 pounds lighter, with short dark brown hair and medium brown eyes. He wore his armor. He approached The Adversary, "Your pride and ego is how you lost. No amount of physical strength can beat a powerful mind. The moment I had both in my possession I won. Mission accomplished."

"This is not over", The Adversary screamed, "Belial!"

CHAPTER THIRTY NINE

The ground shook as in an earthquake. Michael and Uriel glanced at each other. The ground in between The Adversary, Michael, and Uriel opened as Belial flew out of the hole. Once Belial made it out, the ground closed as if never opened.

Belial stood nine feet tall. He had a goat's horn on each side of his head. His appearance was that of half goat and half man. He had goat legs, a human torso, and a half human half goat face with sharp looking teeth; the very image of Baphomet. He held a large mallet in his hand. Leviathan appeared next to him. She was exceedingly beautiful. She stood seven feet tall, black hair with aquamarine blue eyes, sensual looking almond-shaped eyes, with a perfect hour glass shape.

Uriel looked her up and down then mumbled, "How can evil be so beautiful? "Michael elbowed him to make him snap back into reality. No matter how beautiful she was she was their enemy and the wife of Satan.

Thousands of fallen ones appeared encircling the five of them. Michael opened his hand as his flaming sword appeared. The Adversary snarled. He opened his right hand as his trident appeared. He opened his left hand as his sword appeared. Uriel opened his left hand as his spear appeared. He stuck out his right arm as a golden shield appeared on his forearm. The Adversary smirked, "Outnumbered are we?"

Gabriel appeared dressed for battle. He held a golden sword in one hand and the spear of The Father in the other, the same spear Michael used during the first war in heaven that once contained the untranslatable language on it; the very spear that banished Lucifer. The Adversary stared at the spear as he took two steps backwards. Leviathan glanced at Adriana. She had passed out from the sight of all of those fallen ones. Leviathan opened her hand as it illuminated a red hue. She took a step forward towards Michael, Gabriel, and Uriel. She looked at Uriel and said, "For you." She put her opened hand towards her mouth and blew him a kiss. A cloud of fire flew towards him. Uriel shielded himself with his golden shield deflecting it away from him.

Belial firmly gripped his mallet ready to swing at The Adversary's command. The Adversary stared at Leviathan in irritation, "Now who told you to do that?"

She said, "I do as I wish. You have no control over me."

"You wait for my command."

"I do as I wish."

The Adversary shook his head in disapproval then stared at Gabriel, "Gabriel, is there a message for me? Or shall we fight and get this over with."

Gabriel placed his sword in its sling then opened his hand. When he opened his hand, a sealed scroll appeared. The Adversary stared at the scroll in confusion. He said, "Since when does The Father send messages in scrolls?"

Gabriel did not say a word. He held the scroll out for him to grab. The Adversary approached cautiously glancing at all three of them. He grabbed the scroll, broke the seal, and opened it. It read: *When he opened the fifth seal, I saw under the alter the souls of those who had been slain because of the word of God and the testimony they had maintained. They called out in a loud voice, "How long, Sovereign Lord, holy and true, until you judge the inhabitants of the earth and avenge our blood?"...the fifth seal will be opened shortly.*

The Adversary crumbled the scroll as it disappeared in his hand then said, "The fifth seal?"

Gabriel said, "The tribulation."

The Adversary's eyebrows crumbled, "We'll have our time."

Michael said, "Very shortly. You're out of time."

The Adversary stood in front of Michael staring him eye to eye, "This isn't over. I'm bringing the entire world with me. You shall see."

Michael smirked. The Adversary went towards Belial and Leviathan. He said, "I can't wait to see your pain as I murder over 95% of these automatons," he glanced at Belial and Leviathan, "Our time is now. We have 33 earth years before Moses and Elijah return. We must start the grooming process."

Belial and Leviathan nodded in agreement. Belial vanished. Leviathan motioned for the crowd of fallen ones to retreat. They vanished. Leviathan stared at Uriel, "Until we meet again." She smiled, winked then vanished.

The Adversary hurled his Trident at Michael. It vanished before it could hit him.

Michael said, "Useless. There's no war until the seventh seal has been opened. You know that."

The Adversary snarled as he disappeared.

Gabriel glanced at Michael, "Well done." He disappeared.

Uriel touched Michael's shoulder, "How did you know?"

"I didn't. I took a chance. I had no other options so I blew it and hoped for the best."

"You did well."

"Not well enough little brother. Not well enough."

Michael took in a deep breath then exhaled slowly. He approached Sonya's body. He knelt down next to her and wept. After he cried for a few seconds, he said, "I'm so sorry I failed you, but you are forever blessed. I can't wait to see you again. Sleep now."

Uriel said, "We must go."

Michael said, "Hold on." He walked towards Jordin. He peered at her body as tears escaped from his eyes, "Thank you. I've never met a more courageous woman. You will sleep until that great day. I will see you again my friend." Michael knelt down beside her. His hand illuminated as her body straightened out.

He glanced at Adriana as he stood. She had awakened and was getting up off of the ground. They heard police sirens in the distance. She stood frozen unable to believe her own eyes. Michael said, "Darkness. I pity you," He turned towards Uriel, "Ready when you are." They both flew away as the heavens closed behind them. Adriana watched in amazement as they flew away. The police sirens became more audible as she took one last look at Pastor Jones, Sonya, and Jordin's lifeless bodies then grabbed the gun and ran away.

Nicole Michelle

BOOKS BY KENERLY PRESENTS

NEW RELEASE

AVAILABLE IN EBOOK AND PAPERBACK FORMATTING

"I DON'T TRUST YOU"

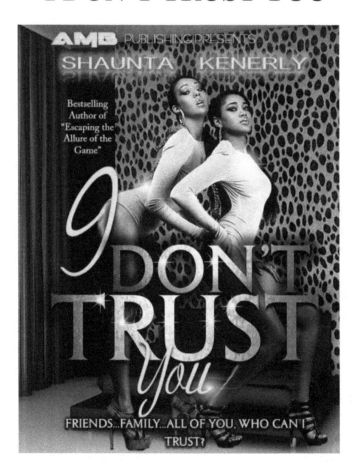

Nicole Michelle

NEW RELEASE

SCI-FI SERIES BOOK AND TELEVISION

AMAZON EXCLUSIVE RELEASE

TRILL BLOOD BY FREE-STYLE

KENERLY PRESENTS

KENERLY PRESENTS

BESTSELLING AUTHOR DANNAYE
CARTER

Nicole Michelle

LIKE MOTHER LIKE TRICK AVAILABLE
NOW

PAPERBACK, NOOK, AND KINDLE

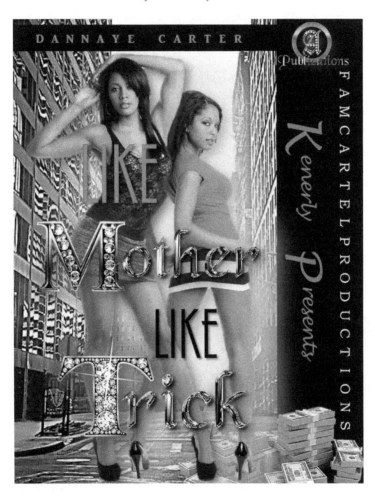

CPSIA information can be obtained
at www.ICGtesting.com
Printed in the USA
LVHW080955130521
687340LV00012B/215